DEADHEAT

Saki Aida

Corvus is a ...
Its name means "crow" in Latin. ...
it depicts a raven. Unlike most constellations, this bird ...
distinctive quadrilateral or cross-shape in the night sky. It's

DEADHEAT

Written by
Saki Aida

Illustrations by
Yuh Takashina

Translated by
Bitter Sweetheart

California and ... recoveries (with ...
a total of 6,727 recoveries ... There were ...
(non-improvised explosive devices (IEDs)). There were ...
... suspicious/unattended package incidents, a decrease of ...

DEADHEAT: DEADLOCK VOLUME TWO is rated MATURE for Intense Violence, Graphic Sexual Content, Strong Language, Horror, Death, Murder, Mature Themes, Blood, Nudity, Sensuality, Racism, and Adult Activities. Reader discretion is advised.

Originally published in Japan in 2006 by TOKUMA SHOTEN PUBLISHING CO, LTD., Tokyo.
English translation rights arranged with TOKUMA SHOTEN PUBLISHING CO, LTD. through Rightol Media.

TRANSLATION: BITTER SWEETHEART
ILLUSTRATIONS: YUH TAKASHINA
COVER and INTERIOR DESIGN: ADDIS
INTERIOR ANIMATION ART: RARA
EDITOR: SOFIA ARANGO
EDITOR-IN-CHIEF: ADDIS

978-1-964533-08-7 HARDBACK
978-1-964533-07-0 PAPERBACK
978-1-964533-12-4 DIGITAL

Printed In Canada
First Printing: 2025

10 9 8 7 6 5 4 3 2 1

Contents

White Heaven

Burnford

Corvus

SAN GABRIEL CEM

CLASSIFIED

FBI OMI

~~Nathan Clark~~

New York

Yuuto Lennix

Schelgar

EVE FILE

CHAPTER 1

New York, New York.

Yuuto Lennix was meeting Jerry Rodriguez at a small café near Chelsea Market. The choice had been his former colleague's, yet as Yuuto neared the red-brick façade, a quiet nostalgia stirred in him. During his DEA days, he had spent countless mornings there.

After nearly ten months away, the neighborhood looked the same at first glance, but subtle changes were noticeable. Across the street, a new Italian restaurant had opened, and even the building next door was painted a different color.

The crisp scent of autumn filled Manhattan as Yuuto quickened his pace, carrying the weight of the time he had been away. Before long, he reached the café. Pushing open the door, he entered the warm, antique charm of the place. At the very back, Jerry was waiting, newspaper in hand.

When Yuuto approached, Jerry stood up from his chair, his face lit with excitement. The two hugged naturally, their reunion warm and genuine.

"Jerry!" Yuuto called out. "Sorry I'm late."

"You look good, Yuuto," Jerry said, waving off the apology.

"You too," Yuuto answered, ordering a cappuccino before sitting down. "Sorry for calling you up out of the blue like that."

Jerry was an easygoing Puerto Rican, two years older than Yuuto and now thirty. After Yuuto's former partner, Paul, Jerry was the person he was closest to.

"Don't mention it, I was glad to hear from you." Jerry smiled warmly. "I've been worried about you this whole time. Seeing you again like this… It's a real relief."

Yuuto smiled, but before he could answer, Jerry spoke again.

"Oh, right! Here's the name and address of the cemetery where Paul is," Jerry said, sliding a note across the table. "It's in Flushing, so it's not too far."

"Thanks," Yuuto said, glancing down at the note. "That helps a lot."

After agreeing to join the FBI to hunt down Corvus, Yuuto traveled to Quantico for the required training. Instead of heading directly to the FBI headquarters in Washington, D.C., after finishing his training, he took a day off to visit Paul's grave in New York. When he called Jerry to ask for the location, Jerry begged to meet if Yuuto was in Manhattan, and Yuuto couldn't refuse.

"Yuuto," Jerry said, leaning forward. "Are you really not planning to come back to the DEA?"

Yuuto shook his head before adding, "Fortunately, I have already secured my next job, so I am ready to start anew."

He kept his tone deliberately light, mentioning only that he had found a job and would be moving to D.C.

"I see. That's really a shame. Everyone was hoping you'd come back, you know?"

Yuuto offered him a faint smile and took a sip from the cup that had just been placed in front of him.

"So, what kind of company is it?"

"A security firm," Yuuto replied after a brief pause.

Jerry nodded without the slightest hint of suspicion. "Got it."

The lie slipped out simply because it was easier. If he told the truth, Jerry would inevitably start digging into the details, and

Yuuto's situation wasn't something that could be explained in a single conversation.

"You've lost a little weight. Things must've been rough for you, huh?"

It was hard to meet Jerry's concerned gaze. Being openly pitied didn't sit well with Yuuto, but he couldn't blame Jerry for it. What else could anyone feel toward a man who'd been falsely thrown in prison?

"It was a rare, once-in-a-lifetime experience," Yuuto said casually, trying to keep the mood from turning heavy. "Not that I'd ever want to go through it again."

"Hey, Yuuto," Jerry said, his voice carrying a hint of hesitation. "If you've got time, you should come see everyone."

"Sorry, but I'm in a hurry," Yuuto replied curtly.

Jerry fell silent, looking awkward, as if he'd understood exactly what Yuuto wasn't saying. A faint pang of guilt tugged at Yuuto, but he still had no desire to see his former colleagues. Just a year ago, he had been an agent at the DEA's New York office. But then, one day, his partner, Paul McClane, was stabbed to death by an unknown assailant—and Yuuto's life was upended.

He was arrested as a suspect and sentenced to fifteen years in prison. He was exonerated after the real killer was caught, but by then, Yuuto had already lost too much.

"Are you still holding a grudge against them?"

Avoiding Jerry's eyes, Yuuto shifted his gaze to the window.

"I get why you're angry," Jerry said quietly. "But back then, none of us were thinking clearly. Can't you forgive us?"

"Jerry. I don't hate anyone. I just want to forget the past, that's all."

While Yuuto was in custody, the only visitors were Jerry and his direct supervisor. Confronted with overwhelming evidence, nearly all of his colleagues believed he was the killer. Even worse, during the trial, one of them testified as a witness for the prosecution.

A White colleague who had been close to Paul testified that the night before the murder, Yuuto and Paul had a heated argument and parted ways on bad terms. And as if that weren't enough, guided by the prosecution's leading questions, he claimed that while Yuuto was usually quiet, he was the kind of man who, when he lost his temper, was capable of anything. The man had likely believed Yuuto was guilty, and in his own misguided way, convinced himself he was helping to get justice for Paul.

Paul had been warm, cheerful, and well-liked by everyone. In contrast, Yuuto, who was poor at socializing, had always been somewhat of an outsider. His arrest rate had been excellent, but that only earned him envy from others. As the only Japanese agent in the DEA office, there had no doubt been a measure of racial bias mixed in with the resentment.

He'd been disappointed in the colleagues who hadn't believed in him, but Yuuto told himself it was his own fault for never building anything beyond surface-level relationships. So he had done his best to forget them all. There was no point in seeing them now. Even if they celebrated his release, they would treat him as if he were fragile glass. It would just feel empty.

"Jerry, tell everyone I said hi. I'm going to live life on my own terms from now on." Yuuto smiled faintly. "I'll make use of my experience at the DEA and keep moving forward."

"Got it." Jerry gave a small, complicated nod. "When you find a place in D.C., give me a call."

"I will," Yuuto replied, though he already knew he probably wouldn't see Jerry again. He liked the man, but being around him only dredged up the past, and that hurt too much.

After parting ways with Jerry in front of the café, Yuuto boarded the Number 1 subway line. He took it to Times Square, transferred to the Number 7 line—the Flushing Local—and got off in Flushing, Queens. From there, hc hailed a cab and instructed the driver to take him to the cemetery.

In just ten minutes, closer than he'd expected, the taxi pulled into a green, tree-filled cemetery. Yuuto asked the driver to wait, then stepped out with the bouquet he'd bought.

The grass lay lush and soothing to the eyes. The sunlight still carried a trace of summer's warmth, yet the breeze hinted at the nearness of autumn. Yuuto squinted against the afternoon glare as he walked through the sprawling cemetery.

Finally, he found Paul's gravestone. When Paul was killed, Yuuto was taken into custody almost immediately, so he hadn't been able to attend the funeral. He had longed to lay flowers on his partner's grave with his own hands, and now, finally, he could. The thought brought him a deep sense of relief.

The small stone marker was embedded in the grass, with Paul's name, birth year, and death year engraved on its face. Yuuto crouched down and traced Paul's name with his fingertips. The moment he did, a hot ache welled up in his chest.

Paul. So this is where you've been. I finally found you...

Yuuto mourned Paul's life, cut tragically short at only thirty-two, as he gently set the bouquet he had brought upon the ground.

"Sorry it took me so long to get here. Not that it's an excuse, but I've been really busy...and trust me, it's not funny." Yuuto spoke as if Paul were really standing right in front of him. This was his last conversation with his partner—the moment he could truly say goodbye. "I really almost died back there, you know? Ever since you've been gone, my life's been a mess. You were supposed to be my partner, damn it! Leaving me to deal with all this alone? I ought to hold a grudge against you for that."

Deep down, he still clung to the foolish hope that Paul might somehow still be alive. He wasn't there when Paul died. He didn't go to the funeral. Worse, he was accused of murdering him. Maybe that's why Yuuto couldn't fully accept his friend's death.

But standing here now, at Paul's grave, he could finally face the truth.

Paul was gone.

And he was no longer part of the DEA.

That day, Yuuto closed the door on his past.

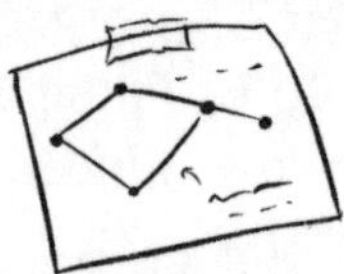

"Think of it as a learner's permit. You understand what I mean, don't you?" Mark Heiden swept a hand through his pale blond hair with a cocky gesture, the kind that implied practiced arrogance. "Your position as an FBI special agent is provisional—for this case only."

Yuuto looked at Heiden's sharply outlined profile and nodded. "I get it. You'll let me drive, but you won't give me the keys to the highway."

"That's right. Honestly, you're still officially a trainee. The only reason you have this title is that we need you for the Corvus investigation. Focus solely on tracking Corvus. If you interfere with anything else, I'll pull you off this case immediately." Heiden's gray eyes fixed on him coldly before he turned and continued down the hallway.

Yuuto followed, tugging his finger between his collar and necktie. *Damn, it's suffocating.*

He'd never liked suits or ties. During his DEA days, he spent most of his time working undercover, far from anything resembling formal attire. Even in his personal life, he only wore suits for special occasions. He always hated restrictive clothing, but now that he's an FBI special agent, he'll have to get used to it.

He'd worked with the FBI a few times during his DEA years,

and every time those so-called "elite" agents swooped in to take over, the field agents—including Yuuto—mocked them behind their backs, calling them "suit guys."

Now, he was one of them. The thought left him with a bitter, complicated feeling.

"What's next?" Yuuto asked. "Do I have to shake hands with anyone else?"

Just two days after completing his training at the academy in Quantico, Yuuto had spent a night in New York before arriving at FBI headquarters in D.C. barely an hour ago. Following a brief, perfunctory self-introduction to the counterterrorism agents who would be his new colleagues, Heiden promptly hauled him through the sprawling building, insisting he greet the higher-ups.

"Your grand tour is over. Come back to my office; we need to discuss what comes next."

Mark Heiden, who was eight years older than Yuuto at thirty-six, would be his direct supervisor from now on. He carried the typical air of a White Anglo-Saxon Protestant, someone raised in privilege. His finely tailored suit, cut from what appeared to be the finest Italian fabric, fit him perfectly. The pretentiousness grated on Yuuto's nerves, but at least Heiden wasn't one of those tacky types who strutted around in cheap navy serge suits while pretending to embody the FBI.

A mocking smile that seemed to look down on everyone else was permanently etched on Heiden's handsome face, signaling a high level of pride. Yuuto didn't like him, but Heiden probably felt the same about him. After all, he was forced to accept a prisoner he had once interrogated as his subordinate. Yuuto had heard it was the FBI's higher-ups who insisted on bringing him on board as an agent.

Once in his office, Heiden ordered a junior agent to bring coffee. The young agent glanced at Yuuto with a meaningful look before leaving the room. Yuuto noticed the same flicker in the eyes of other agents when they looked at him. He faced the reality that he was an unwanted presence, but it was exactly what he'd expected.

Even if his conviction had been overturned, the fact remained that he was an ex-convict turned FBI special agent. The backlash was only natural. Typically, it takes four rigorous months of academy training, plus more than a year of observation, to become an FBI agent. Yet Yuuto had completed only a token month of training before being put on active investigations. He understood without it needing to be said that this was an extraordinary exception.

Heiden pulled a thick file from his desk drawer, dropped it, and effectively snapped him out of his thoughts.

"This file contains the investigation status on a series of bombings. Dates and locations of the attacks, damage reports, types of bombs used, and other details. Reviewing it will give you a good idea of what we currently know. Take a look."

Since last year, a series of seemingly random bombings has terrorized the United States. Because no group claimed responsibility, the public dubbed them "Silent terrorism," spreading fear and anxiety nationwide.

The attacks spanned states from Utah, Arizona, Montana, Michigan, to Florida, with no clear pattern in target locations—supermarkets, hospitals, office buildings, schools, and train stations had all been hit.

Earlier this year, the FBI unexpectedly arrested a man believed to be involved in a series of attacks. The suspect admitted to being part of a cult and said that the leader ordered all actions.

However, he was fatally shot while being transferred to FBI headquarters. Before dying, he revealed a critical detail: the cult's leader, known to his followers as Corvus—Latin for "crow"—was hiding in plain sight as an inmate at Schelger State Prison in California, and from within those walls, he continued to direct his followers, orchestrating the attacks.

When the FBI discovered this, they made a special plea deal with Yuuto, who was in prison. If he could locate Corvus within Schelger, they promised to release him. For Yuuto, this was his only hope. He didn't want to spend fifteen years in prison for a crime he didn't commit. Without hesitation, he accepted the deal and was transferred to Schelger.

The only clues he had were that Corvus was about thirty years old, suspected of murder, had received formal military training, and bore a large burn scar on his back. Using just that limited information, Yuuto searched the prison.

Eventually, he uncovered the truth: the model prisoner who had treated him kindly, a man named Nathan Clark, was actually Corvus. Though Corvus managed to escape in the end, Yuuto used his trump card—the contact he had with Corvus—to negotiate his own release.

The FBI, feeling pressured by the CIA's lead in the case, found evidence to clear Yuuto's name and legally release him. They planned to use Yuuto—the only person to have ever come into contact with the mysterious Corvus—in their ongoing investigation.

Heiden, sitting on the edge of his desk, asked, "How was the training at the academy?"

Yuuto, sitting on the sofa and flipping through the file, took a sip of coffee and shrugged. "The place brought back memories. It reminded me of the hellish DEA training I went through back in the day."

"Right. The DEA academy was also in Quantico, wasn't it?"

Quantico was home to a massive Marine Corps base. Technically, the town of Quantico was located within the base's extensive grounds, which is why checkpoints guarded its entrances, creating an intimidating atmosphere. Both the FBI and DEA academies were situated on the base, where rookies underwent tough, military-style training to become agents.

As Yuuto nodded, Heiden continued.

"You were an exceptional student, excelling in intelligence, physical fitness, and marksmanship. There were no issues with the mindset expected of an investigator. Your instructors confirmed you were ready for fieldwork right away. Given your record at the DEA, it was evident from the start that you were an outstanding agent. You played a key role in dealing a heavy blow to the *Recabada*."

The *Recabada* was a drug trafficking organization that Yuuto infiltrated years ago. Closely connected to a major Mexican cartel, they smuggled and distributed large amounts of narcotics across the U.S. The DEA had struggled for years to understand the organization's full scope. Yuuto and Paul had spent over a year deep undercover, successfully identifying the group's leader. As a result, most of the leadership was arrested, and the *Recabada* was pushed to the brink of collapse.

But this drastically changed Yuuto and Paul's fate. One of the leaders who had escaped arrest realized that the two were actually undercover agents and that they had been completely deceived. Driven by revenge, he planned to kill Paul and frame Yuuto for the crime. The truth eventually came to light thanks to the FBI, but sloppy police work had played right into the hands of the culprit.

"Didn't the FBI know from the beginning that I wasn't the one who killed Paul?" Yuuto asked.

Otherwise, the real culprit wouldn't have conveniently appeared just when they demanded his release.

"No way," Heiden said, knitting his brows as if insulted. "We worked desperately to prove your innocence."

Yuuto looked down at Heiden's polished shoes. *Not a speck of dust,* he thought absent-mindedly. *He only gave orders and never did any legwork himself.*

"Because you suspected people in *Recabada*, narrowing down suspects was easier. The FBI had been investigating that organization for some time." Heiden's voice softened in a patronizing way, as if telling Yuuto to stop complaining. "Our intelligence network isn't something to overlook, you know?"

It wouldn't be accurate to say Yuuto had no resistance to working for an organization that tried to use him. But regardless of the truth, he chose to compartmentalize and focus on pursuing Corvus with the FBI's resources.

When Yuuto silently nodded, Heiden offered a relieved, emotionless smile. Their attention went back to the file.

The FBI profilers were exceptional, and Yuuto expected to find an analysis of Corvus among their work. But as he flipped through the pages, there was nothing.

"What about the profiling of the actual perpetrator?" he asked.

"The profiling was halted once we realized it wasn't just a lone wolf. My team continues investigating domestic cult groups, but unfortunately, the FBI has never confirmed the existence of an organization called White Heaven, either in the past or present."

White Heaven was the name of the armed cult group Corvus once led, but whether the terrorists working as Corvus's operatives were remnants of White Heaven or a completely new group remained unknown.

"Maybe they changed their name and went underground?" Yuuto suggested. "They definitely existed. Two years ago, there was a White Heaven siege in South Carolina, and the army was mobilized."

Heiden rubbed his forehead, looking pained. "When I checked with the Pentagon, they denied any such incident. I used my personal connections to investigate the army's involvement. Apparently, the deployment was an unofficial military order."

"Sounds like the Pentagon doesn't want to acknowledge White

Heaven publicly?"

"If that's the case, it's a real headache. If the military acted in secret, there could be political motives involved."

Political motives.

For those working on the ground in investigations, that was by far the most troublesome interference.

"So, this past month, while I was at the academy, did you uncover anything new?" Yuuto tried to shift the mood, hoping there had been progress in the case thanks to the information he'd provided.

But Heiden's answer only brought disappointment.

"Unfortunately, nothing concrete," he said with a shake of his head. "We still have no solid leads on Corvus, wanted under the name Nathan Clark. We collected fingerprints and hair samples believed to be his from the cell where he was held, but there was no match in the FBI database. And Richard Corning, the warden of Schelger Prison who is suspected of helping Corvus escape, has been missing since the riot."

Since Corning was thought to have close ties to Corvus, finding him could lead to a major breakthrough. Yuuto had hoped for that, so the news hit him hard.

"We also investigated the real Nathan Clark's background, but nothing suspicious came up."

Yuuto looked thoughtfully at the photos of bomb sites pinned in the file. The extent of destruction varied greatly. Some blasts left only holes in walls; others nearly destroyed entire buildings. Most of the attacks happened late at night or early in the morning when no one was around. Considering the scale, the relatively low number of casualties was a small mercy.

"What do you think happened to the real Nathan?" Yuuto asked, looking up.

"Most likely, he's been killed. Having two identical men

around would only make things more complicated."

"I don't think Nathan was chosen as a random scapegoat. He probably had some connection to Corvus in the past."

"Do you have any proof of that?"

"No proof, but Corvus isn't the kind of man who acts on a whim." Corvus had gained deep trust among the inmates. Even Yuuto, who had gotten close to him, was completely fooled by his act and had come to genuinely respect the man.

"I know it's frustrating, but you must endure. Losing your temper won't do you any favors."

"...you need to stay away from the bad influences here. Be a model prisoner, and work hard to get out as soon as possible."

Nathan had always spoken to him with kindness and encouragement. Whenever Yuuto thought of Corvus, the face of that gentle Nathan kept flashing through his mind. Although he knew the truth, the image of the brutal terrorist still didn't quite match the kind man he had come to know.

But that was precisely what made Corvus terrifying. To hide in plain sight as a model prisoner for two whole years demanded patience and mental strength, coupled with the cunning and skill to wear the mask of a good man—qualities that stood in stark contrast to his true nature. Even that alone was enough to mark him as no ordinary man.

Heiden raised an eyebrow with a look that practically said, *Well, well.*

"Figures. You did live in close quarters with Corvus for a while. Seems like you know him pretty well."

Yuuto didn't fall for it. Instead, he tapped his finger on the file. "These bombings might look random, but I think there's a pattern. Some kind of intent behind them, at least from his perspective."

"Intent?" Heiden's voice was sharp with disbelief. "There's nothing consistent about any of it. The man lacks principles or ideology—he's simply a thrill-seeker. He creates chaos to satisfy that dirty craving for attention, nothing more." Heiden spat the words out like they tasted bitter. "Lennix. I have no patience for people like that. Motive or not, I will never tolerate terrorism. No matter what it takes, I'll see that bastard Corvus behind bars. Trust me."

He'd always seemed like the type who only cared about climbing the career ladder, but it turned out Heiden did have a sense of resolve as an investigator. The realization eased Yuuto's mind a little, and he nodded.

"Agreed."

"Oh, and one more thing," Heiden added. "Your old cellmate—Dick Burnford. Or rather, the man pretending to be him. He was a contracted CIA agent."

The sudden mention of Dick's name threw Yuuto off balance. He didn't let it show, but his heart rate spiked.

"What about Dick?"

"Nothing on the man himself. However, the real Burnford apparently died while serving time in another prison. The CIA pulled some strings, made it look like he was still alive, and arranged to have him transferred to Schelger Prison. Somewhere along the line, he got replaced."

Replacing a man completely…that wasn't something you could do easily. It would've required manipulating half the federal and judicial system to make it happen.

"The CIA might be planning to assassinate Corvus, but I'll be damned if I let that happen," Heiden went on. "They can play their spy games overseas all they want, but this is U.S. soil. Here, they play by our rules."

Then Heiden's mouth curved into a sharp, unpleasant smile. "We've planted a mole inside CIA headquarters. Even so, Corvus is such a high priority for them that security is tight—we can't get a clear read on their internal movements. But one thing's certain: they haven't found him yet either."

That was the most helpful thing Yuuto had heard all day.

"Lennix," Heiden said, leaning back in his chair. "Whether it's law enforcement, politics, or business, the side with the most information wins. Remember that. Information is the key to everything."

There was a dangerous glint in Heiden's eyes, one that showed a hint of hatred. He probably had been burned by the CIA before—outsmarted, humiliated.

The rivalry between the two agencies chasing Corvus wasn't something that formed overnight. It had been built up and intensified over time through history. No matter how many personnel exchanges they arranged or how many joint task forces they created, the deep-rooted tension between them wasn't something that could be easily smoothed over.

The CIA—an intelligence agency reporting directly to the President—focused on overseas operations and espionage. The FBI, under the Department of Justice, was charged with policing domestic crime. Spies for the CIA. Spy-hunters for the FBI. Their rivalry was more than a turf war. It shaped America's history from the shadows.

But none of that mattered. Yuuto didn't really care about the FBI's grudge against the CIA.

CHAPTER 2

That day, his only task was his discussion with Heiden. Afterwards, he received his FBI badge, ID card, and service pistol, then he left the Bureau's headquarters.

The moment he stepped onto the sidewalk, an Asian woman clutching a Japanese travel guide spoke to him in hesitant English.

"Ekuuse me…ah, you Japanesu?"

When someone who seemed Japanese asked if he was Japanese, it always felt a little awkward. The truth was complicated. His passport was American, and by blood, he wasn't fully Japanese either. His late mother had been half-White, which technically made him a quarter.

"I'm Japanese-American," he said.

"*Eeto…Nihongo wa hanasemasuka?*"

"Um, *sukoshinara*."

The woman asked if he spoke Japanese, and she looked relieved when he replied that he did speak a little. She seemed lost and clearly didn't know where she was.

"You're here." Yuuto leaned in, glanced at her map, and began explaining the area to her in Japanese. "If you keep going straight down this street, you'll reach the White House. From there, if you turn left at the next block, you'll find your hotel."

"Thank you. That really helps!"

Washington, D.C., was a popular tourist destination. The White House, the Lincoln Memorial, the Capitol Building, and the Smithsonian museums—all the major landmarks—were clustered within the same area, drawing visitors not only from across the country but also from around the world. The FBI headquarters was once a tourist attraction. Prior to 9/11, the building offered tours that drew long lines of eager visitors.

Terrorism could never be justified, no matter the reason.

Yuuto didn't know Corvus's goal, but one thing was clear—he had to capture him before the next attack. And for that, he needed information.

"Information is the key to everything." Heiden's words from earlier flickered through his mind.

"Information, huh?" Yuuto murmured under his breath as he headed west on E Street. Ahead was the White House—the President's residence.

As he walked, Yuuto looked up at the FBI headquarters next to him. Officially, it was called the J. Edgar Hoover Building, named after the man who had become Director at twenty-nine and led the Bureau for nearly fifty years.

Hoover served eight presidents and was rumored to have manipulated each from behind the scenes. Some mocked him as a master of blackmail, but his true weapon was the information he had collected through surveillance. However, information alone had no power. Only the ability to analyze and use it gave it real value.

When Yuuto was with the DEA, his days were consumed by collecting intelligence on drug cases. Sometimes he'd posed as a junkie to approach dealers. Other times, he'd gone undercover as a seller himself to infiltrate trafficking rings. It had been dangerous work, but with enough experience, the rules and structure of the drug world had started to make sense to him.

But none of that would help him now. This investigation was an entirely different world. He couldn't afford to overlook even the smallest lead. He would have to strip away preconceptions, analyze every detail, and move with caution.

Could he really do it?

Could he deliver results?

Even with determination, a vague unease followed him like a shadow. It felt like setting sail alone into a vast ocean. When he was sent to Schelger State Prison, he was anxious then too—but at least back then, he quickly found allies. Matthew, with his boyish face and innocence; Mickey, cheerful and talkative, always looking out for others; Nathan, calm and steady, whose quiet presence was a comfort; and Dick—cold and distant, yet the one who had saved him more than once.

Yuuto pushed those thoughts aside and picked up his pace. He didn't have time to waste. He needed to find a place to stay. When he'd been sentenced, his lease was canceled, and now he was effectively homeless. He spent the afternoon visiting several real estate offices, but nothing matched his criteria. By the fourth office, he gave up, deciding there was no point in rushing, and headed back to his hotel.

That evening, Yuuto stopped at a small restaurant near the hotel for dinner. After placing his order, he stood up to grab a newspaper from the stand near the entrance. As he stepped into the aisle, his shoulder brushed against someone passing by.

"Oh, sorry," Yuuto quickly apologized and turned around—only to feel his heart skip a beat. The man he'd bumped into was a tall White guy.

"No problem," the man said with a friendly smile before slipping past him.

Yuuto returned to his table with a copy of *The Washington Post* in hand and started flipping through it. But his eyes weren't focused on the words. Instead, he kept sneaking glances at the man from earlier. The stranger sat in the back, chatting casually with another man. His perfect blond hair and sharp, handsome face reminded Yuuto of Dick. The man was good-looking, no doubt—but he wasn't Dick.

Yuuto closed the paper and let out a quiet sigh.

"Forget about me. That's what's best for you."

Those words—and the pained look in Dick's eyes as he spoke them—still pierced Yuuto's chest every time he remembered.

Dick was twenty-nine, just a year older than Yuuto, and he commanded a certain respect among the other inmates. He had striking blue eyes, clear as a mountain lake, and hair so perfectly blond it almost gleamed.

Yuuto's first impression of him had been terrible.

On the very first day in prison, Dick had looked him over and declared flatly, "*In here, you're clearly prey.*" Then, just to drive it home, he'd added, *"I've got no interest in cleaning up after some dumb newbie."*

Yuuto hated him for it. That cold, dismissive attitude had been infuriating. But over time, the distance between them shrank. And before Yuuto realized it, he'd been drawn in—irresistibly. Beneath Dick's icy exterior, there was a quiet kindness, a lonely figure who carried himself with a dignity that almost hurt to look at. The more Yuuto learned, the deeper he fell under that spell.

Then came the prison riots—an all-out war between the Black and Chicano gangs that tore the place apart. In the chaos, Yuuto uncovered two devastating truths: Nathan, his calm and steady friend, had been Corvus all along. And Dick…Dick was a CIA assassin sent to kill him.

When Corvus finally removed his mask and tried to kill them both, Yuuto and Dick barely escaped, only saved because the gang war had broken out nearby. They ran through the chaos and ended up in the prison's food storage, where Dick finally told Yuuto about his past.

Dick used to be a Delta Force operative in the Army's elite

counterterrorism unit—until a mission went terribly wrong. Corvus slaughtered his team. His lover. Everyone. From that day forward, Dick lived for revenge. He signed a deal with the CIA, becoming their weapon for one purpose: to kill Corvus.

That was all he had left. His reason for living.

And Yuuto had ruined it.

He had gotten in the way, and Dick's one chance had slipped away. But when Corvus escaped during the riots, Dick didn't hesitate. He seized the chaos to break out of prison and disappear into the outside world.

At first, he asked Yuuto to come with him, but he refused. He wanted to go. *God, he really wanted to go.* But that wouldn't have meant freedom. It would have been a life on the run, branded a fugitive, hiding forever.

So when the FBI came for him, offering him a chance to join their ranks, Yuuto didn't hesitate. He said yes without a second thought, because it gave him a way to keep chasing the same man Dick was after.

As long as he was on the same trail…there was a chance. A chance he might see Dick again.

That filthy little room they'd hidden in during the riots came back to Yuuto like it had happened only yesterday. Cornered by the inevitability of their parting, the two of them had reached for each other without thought, stripped of pretense and lies. It had been raw and desperate, as if they were searching for the unvarnished truth inside each other—speaking in the heat of skin, in the depth of desire, in a language only they could understand.

"I want to take you with me. I don't want to let you go."

Yuuto believed those words with all his heart. They revealed Dick's true feelings—he didn't doubt it, because they reflected his own. When they were forced to part, it felt like his heart was being torn in two.

If they'd never crossed that line—if they'd never held each other—maybe Yuuto could have written Dick off as just a cellmate he'd shared a few months with. But they had crossed it. They had shared something real. They had given each other a love so deep it still ached in Yuuto's chest.

Yuuto wasn't gay. But in his entire life, he had never felt that way about anyone else. He could pretend to forget, bury himself in the day-to-day grind, lose himself in work, and eventually the past would blur, growing distant and faint. But he didn't want to forget. He didn't want to turn Dick into just another memory.

When he thought of Dick out there somewhere, still suffering and living only for the chance to kill Corvus, Yuuto couldn't sit still.

There was a reason the FBI recruited him. The connection between him and Dick hadn't been broken. It was still there. He could feel it, and he wanted to believe in it. He refused to let this opportunity slip away. He would follow that invisible thread with everything he had, no matter where it led.

Dick...I'm coming for Corvus, too.

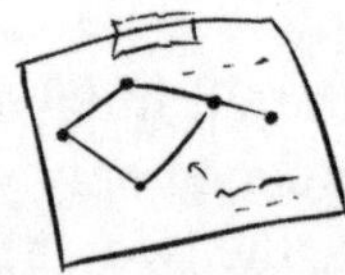

The next morning, Yuuto had barely arrived at work when Heiden called him in.

"We received a call from the FBI's Los Angeles field office."

"Bad news?" Yuuto asked. From Heiden's stiff tone alone, he could tell it wasn't good.

Heiden shot him a grim look and nodded. "The worst. They found Corning."

They had finally found their main person of interest—yet somehow, it was the worst-case scenario.

There could be only one reason for that.

"He's dead?" Yuuto asked.

"Yeah," Heiden confirmed. "They pulled his body from a car at the bottom of the ocean. He was shot. What do you make of it?"

"Corvus," Yuuto answered without hesitation. "He used Corning to get out of prison—and then killed him to keep him quiet. That's the only plausible scenario I can see."

Heiden gave a slow nod as he set his coffee cup down on the table.

"Heiden. Let me go to L.A.," Yuuto said.

"L.A.? Why?" Heiden arched a doubtful brow. "The LAPD is already handling the Corning case. You showing up won't change anything."

"It's not just about Corning," Yuuto countered. "I want to dig into Nathan's background while I'm there. There has to be a connection to Corvus somewhere. And I want to visit Schelger Prison. I might find a lead there."

Heiden fell silent, clearly considering his options. Yuuto noticed the hesitation in his face—he wasn't comfortable with the idea of sending a rookie out alone.

"Why do you think they brought me into the FBI under special exception?" Yuuto pressed. "If this were just about canvassing bomb sites or tracking down parts used in explosives, any other agent could handle it. But with this case, there are things only I can do. So let me go to L.A."

Heiden studied him for a moment, then gave a quiet nod. "You have a point. Honestly, I haven't expected much from you. If all you could do were the same work as everyone else, I'd already be sending you back to the academy. But maybe this is a good opportunity."

"So…you'll let me go?" Yuuto asked.

"Yeah. But you've got three days," Heiden said. "If you can't find anything in three days, I want you back here immediately."

Yuuto wasn't confident he could find new leads in just three days. But he had no choice—*he had to try.*

"I'll put in a request with the LAPD to cooperate with you. Can you leave now?"

"I'll head out right away," Yuuto replied.

"Good. I authorize you to carry out this investigation on your own."

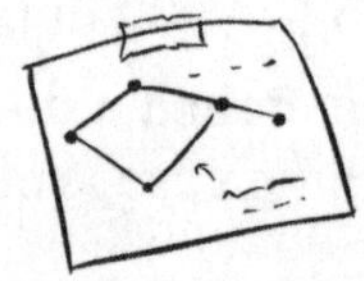

The flight lasted nearly five hours before the plane finally touched down at Los Angeles International Airport. Though Yuuto had been living in New York for the past decade, returning to his hometown never failed to bring him a sense of calm. Stepping off at Terminal 7 for domestic arrivals, he started walking toward the exit.

"Yuuto! Over here!"

He turned toward the booming voice and saw a man with sun-kissed skin and dark sunglasses standing by the crowd. Dressed sharply in a suit, he strode toward Yuuto with the same confident air he'd always had. Yuuto couldn't help but smile and wave in greeting.

It was Francisco "Paco" Lennix—his Chicano stepbrother, three years his senior, a homicide detective with the LAPD. Tall, lean, and almost unfairly handsome, Paco was the sort of man Yuuto had always admired, in every sense.

"¡Yuuto! *¿Qué onda?*" Paco greeted him with a wide grin and immediately grabbed Yuuto's bag from his hand. "*¿Cómo estás?*"

Yuuto had called ahead to say he was coming, but he hadn't expected Paco to pick him up in person.

"*Todo bien*," Yuuto replied with a faint smile.

Paco was fluent in English, but whenever just the two of them were together, they always switched back to Spanish—a habit that had never really disappeared.

"Didn't think we'd be seeing each other again so soon," Paco said. "You think you'll have time to visit Leti and the others?"

Yuuto shook his head. "I don't know. I'd love to, but…if I can't, I'd rather not get Lupita's hopes up. Don't tell her I'm here, okay?"

He longed to see his stepmother and little sister, but this was a work trip. A detour to Arizona probably wasn't possible.

"Got it. If she finds out her favorite brother is in L.A., she'll go crazy. She's twelve now, but she's still the same little crybaby."

Yuuto chuckled softly, recalling the last time he saw her. Just a month ago, Lupita had clung to him, tear-stained and pleading, begging him not to leave.

His father remarried when Yuuto was ten, marrying Leticia, Paco's mother. At first, it felt strange to suddenly have a Mexican family. But Leti was warm and kind, and Paco was a bright, good-natured kid who looked out for him. When Lupita was born, their family of four felt complete.

His father passed away two years ago in an accident, but Yuuto had never felt alone. Even though he only saw them a few times a year, Paco, Leti, and Lupita were his family.

"I parked in the lot. Let's go," Paco said.

"You're on duty, right?" Yuuto asked. "Is it okay for you to just sneak out like this?"

"What are you talking about?" Paco smirked and clapped Yuuto on the shoulder. "This is part of my job. I'm here to welcome an FBI agent, after all. Direct orders from the chief, so don't even think about feeling guilty."

"Seriously? Well…if you say so," Yuuto replied, his expression lighting up as he looked at Paco.

With Paco around, he felt like things might actually go smoothly.

"How about we grab something to eat before heading to the station? You've got to be hungry. My treat—let's hit a restaurant."

"An In-N-Out drive-thru's fine," Yuuto answered immediately.

Paco raised his eyebrows, half-exasperated. "Burgers? Man, you've loved that place forever."

"They're way better than McDonald's or Burger King," Yuuto said with a grin. "I can only get it when I'm out here, so let me enjoy it."

In-N-Out was a fast-food chain exclusively in California, Arizona, and Nevada—and Yuuto loved their burgers more than anything else.

"Órale," Paco laughed. "Fine. Your wish is my command."

He reached over and ruffled Yuuto's black hair before flashing a wide, toothy grin.

They ate their burgers in the car, then spent almost an hour crawling through L.A.'s infamous traffic before finally arriving at the LAPD headquarters. The station was located on the east side of downtown, right near the iconic City Hall that appeared in countless movies.

Following Paco's lead, Yuuto entered the busy detective division. First, he met Paco's boss, Section Chief Haig, and thanked him for his help with the investigation. Then, Paco introduced him to the rest of the team.

Most of them, already knowing Yuuto was Paco's younger brother, greeted him warmly. But one man in particular—Mike

Howard, a Black detective—stood out. He was especially friendly, chatting like they'd known each other for years. From the way he spoke, it was clear he and Paco were close, and Mike seemed to know plenty about Yuuto too.

"Yuuto, you should write a memoir someday," Mike said with a grin. "I'm telling you, it'd sell. There isn't another guy in the whole damn country who's been through the DEA, prison, and the FBI."

Yuuto laughed as the cheerful Mike teased him about his background.

"Good idea," he said with a smile. "When I write my memoir someday, I'll make sure to include a capable detective named Mike Howard at the LAPD."

"Hey, Paco! Your little brother's a good guy," Mike called out.

"Yeah, he takes after me," Paco said with a grin. "Alright, Yuuto, let's start with the Richard Corning case."

Before Yuuto arrived, Paco had already gathered information on Corning's murder. He pulled out some documents from a clear file and handed them over.

"By the way, why did Corning help Nathan Clark?"

It was natural for Paco to wonder why a prison warden would help a prisoner escape.

"I'm not sure. All I know is that they had a personal connection."

Under Heiden's orders, neither Paco nor the LAPD had been given all the details. They were only told that Nathan Clark, the prisoner who escaped from Schelger Prison, was suspected of involvement in a series of bombings across the United States and that they were tracking his location. Paco assumed that was why Yuuto had been recruited by the FBI.

"Corning's body was discovered yesterday afternoon at the pier on Terminal Island."

Terminal Island was a port roughly twenty-five miles south of downtown Los Angeles, situated near the border between San Pedro and Long Beach.

"San Pedro police officers discovered it. They had sent divers following reports that a handgun used in another robbery had been discarded nearby. That's when the divers unexpectedly found a car sunk on the seafloor."

"Corning's body was inside?"

"Yeah. The car belonged to Corning himself. The autopsy showed he'd been dead for about a month, maybe six weeks. A gunshot to the head killed him instantly, and afterward the car—with the body inside—was dumped into the sea."

The photos in the documents showed the recovered car and Corning's belongings. Yuuto studied them carefully, brushing his thumb across his lips.

"That gunshot wound to the head…was fired at close range?"

"Yeah, that's what they said."

"The bullet entered on the right side of the temple?"

"Exactly. How did you figure that out?"

It was mostly a gut feeling, but Yuuto had a vague picture forming in his mind. After helping with the prison break, Corvus must have driven them to the port. Sitting in the passenger seat, he'd pressed a gun to Corning's temple—the same gun he'd used on Yuuto and Dick, gripped tightly in his hand, with a faint smirk on his lips. Corning probably never dreamed that the man he'd helped would be the one to kill him.

"It'll be tough to get any eyewitness info there," Yuuto said.

Paco nodded and shrugged off his jacket. "Yeah, that sounds about right. The place isn't popular to begin with, and it's already been a month. Still, the San Pedro station's on the case, so if anything new comes up, they'll report it. If you want, I can take you out there now."

"No, I'll leave that to the local cops. What I really want to know is about Nathan Clark."

"Alright, leave it to me." For some reason, it was Mike who responded eagerly. He placed the file he'd been holding on the desk and opened it with a proud grin. "I worked on the Nathan Clark case two years ago. Ask me anything you want."

Paco sat down in a chair and lit a cigarette, passing the conversation to Mike.

"Do you remember Nathan?" Yuuto asked.

"Not really, to be honest. I remembered the case, but the guy himself didn't leave much of an impression. When I looked back at the files, I just thought, 'Oh, that's him.' He was decent enough—turned himself in, behaved well. There was plenty of circumstantial evidence, so the indictment came quickly."

"He turned himself in?"

"Yeah. He went to his mother's place with no money. She kicked him out cold, and in a fit of rage, he fired the gun he had. Then he panicked and turned himself in right away. No prior record—just spooked."

That story was nothing like what Yuuto had heard inside the prison. Corvus, aware of Yuuto's background, must have fabricated the lie on the spot. By claiming he was a falsely accused victim—framed by the police, grieving someone important—he had sought to win Yuuto's trust through shared experience. And the plan had worked.

Yuuto recalled the seemingly sincere, sympathetic eyes that had met his then, and he had to admit that Corvus had been quite the actor.

"How reliable was that confession?" Yuuto asked.

"There was nothing suspicious. He had the murder weapon when he was arrested. It was definitely Nathan's doing. Nathan had lived alone with his mother, but they had a bad relationship, and he ran away as a young man. He drifted around the U.S. and then returned to L.A. about six months before the incident. He was short on cash, so when he went to visit his mother after all those years, she called him a bastard, and he snapped."

As Yuuto flipped through the investigation files, a photo from Nathan's arrest caught his eye. In the picture, it was clearly Corvus. By that point, Corvus had already impersonated Nathan. The real question was when the switch had happened.

"I want to meet people who knew Nathan before his arrest."

Mike frowned, pulling the files closer. He sighed and started flipping through the pages. If Nathan had turned himself in right after the crime, the investigation would have finished quickly with the confession and physical evidence. There'd be no need to dig into his social circle.

"If you can find out where he was living at the time, I'll go ask around myself," Yuuto said.

"He was homeless," Mike replied. "Ah, wait, wait a sec."

Mike jogged over to his desk and came back carrying a thick binder. The old binder was filled with dozens of pages of cramped, handwritten text.

"What's that?" Yuuto asked.

"My precious work diary." Mike grinned. "I keep it so I can remember later who I met and where I went."

"Wow, you actually keep something like that? Didn't expect you to be so meticulous," Paco muttered in surprise.

Mike puckered his lips.

"What's that supposed to mean? You're supposed to be my friend! How little attention have you been paying to me?" Grumbling, Mike pointed to a section in the notebook. "Look here. It states that immediately after Nathan's arrest, someone requested a meeting. Back then, no one except the lawyer was allowed to see him, so the guy left without meeting Nathan. That guy said he was an acquaintance of Nathan's. Name's…here it is. Rob Connors. The address is even listed."

Yuuto thanked Mike and jotted down Rob Connors's address in his notebook. Suddenly, a shout cut across the room—a burly detective called out, "Paco! Joe Evanson just showed up. Harry and Lacy spotted him and are tailing him."

Paco and Mike exchanged glances and rushed toward the detective, who was holding the radio handset.

"Where is he now? Where did he go?"

"Last seen entering the Figueroa Hotel. Shall we send backup?"

"Absolutely. That bastard's getting caught this time, and I'm gonna throw him in jail for good," Mike said, pumping his clenched fist in excitement.

When Paco returned with an apologetic look, Yuuto spoke up first. "Go ahead. I'm fine on my own. I'll go see this Rob Connors."

"Sorry about that. He's been chasing a murder suspect for a while now…If anything happens, call me right away, got it?" Paco gave Yuuto a light, concerned pat on the cheek.

Yuuto smiled wryly. "I'm good. Now go on—Mike's waiting."

Paco nodded, snatched up his jacket, and set off with Mike at a brisk pace.

CHAPTER 3

Pasadena was famous for the Rose Parade and Rose Bowl held every New Year's Day, but it was also known as one of the wealthiest residential areas, alongside Beverly Hills and Santa Monica. With its retro streets lined with modern shops and a reputation for safety, it was one of the most desirable neighborhoods in the region.

Yuuto stepped out of the taxi in a quiet neighborhood and looked at Rob's house from the street. It wasn't very large, but it had a calm and tidy appearance. A Ford SUV and a popular Toyota Camry were parked neatly in the garage, and the lawn was carefully trimmed, with every part of the yard neatly maintained.

He walked up the short stairs and stopped on the porch. When he pressed the doorbell, the door opened after a moment, and a White man peeked out.

"Who are you?"

The man stifled a yawn as if Yuuto had interrupted his nap and looked at him with sleepy eyes. He appeared to be in his mid-thirties and was about a fist taller than Yuuto—roughly six-foot-one. His hair and eyes were light brown. Although he wore faded jeans and a wrinkled shirt, he didn't look sloppy. His clean, well-groomed features likely contributed to his tidy appearance.

"Are you Rob Connors?"

"Yeah. And you are?"

Yuuto took out his badge holder and flipped it open, revealing his ID.

"FBI?"

FBI

"That's right. Yuuto Lennix, special agent. I'm sorry to bother you, but I have a few questions I'd like to ask. Could I have a moment of your time?"

Rob ran his hand through his slightly wavy hair and let out a small sigh. "Sorry, but I'm done cooperating with you people. Go home."

He started to close the door, but Yuuto instinctively pressed a hand against it to stop him.

"Wait. What do you mean by 'cooperating'? I just want to ask you about someone." Speaking quickly, Yuuto fixed his eyes on Rob. "You know Nathan Clark, don't you?"

"Nathan Clark?" The man frowned, clearly puzzled.

"Yes. He was arrested by the LAPD two years ago for killing his mother. You went all the way to the station back then and asked to see him, didn't you?"

"I did. So what?"

"Nathan was imprisoned in Schelger Prison. During the riots, he escaped."

"Ah. So that's what this is about. If you came here to ask me where Nathan is now, you're wasting your time," Rob said flatly, nodding slowly, as if the pieces had just clicked into place. "I have no idea where he is. I wasn't even that close to him. The only reason I went to the police to see him was out of professional interest."

That explanation made Yuuto pause. What kind of job would seek out a murderer? "Forgive me, but… what do you do for a living?"

"Are you really with the FBI?" Rob asked, suspicion flickering in his eyes.

Yuuto gave a wry smile. "If you doubt me, you're welcome to call the Bureau and confirm it yourself."

"You're from the Los Angeles field office, right? I've never seen you around. Are you new?"

If Rob had some connection to the FBI, that would explain his familiarity with the organization. Still, if he turned out to be a journalist, that could be troublesome. Yuuto made a mental note to tread carefully.

"I am new," Yuuto admitted, "but I'm not with the L.A. office. I'm assigned to headquarters."

"Headquarters? You came all the way from D.C.?"

Yuuto nodded.

Rob looked genuinely surprised, but finally, he appeared to accept Yuuto's credentials and revealed his own. "I'm a criminologist at the University of California. I've helped the FBI a few times in the past, but honestly? Most of the agents I've dealt with don't listen to a word I say after asking for my advice. I got sick of it."

Now it made sense. That was why he'd said he didn't want to cooperate anymore.

"I'm not here to ask you about Nathan's whereabouts," Yuuto said. "I just want to know what kind of man he was. That's all."

"You're not interested in where he is?" Rob arched his brow. "I really don't get you."

He smiled in mild amusement, a smile so effortlessly charming it was hard not to return. Something about him reminded Yuuto of Paco, a man with a boyish streak beneath his mature exterior, the kind of man women probably fell for without him even trying.

"Sorry," Rob said, still smiling, "but I don't want to talk to anyone about Nathan. Try somewhere else."

Even with that simple expression, his refusal stayed firm. He looked gentle, but his tone carried a stubbornness. And if his words were any clue, he really didn't want to deal with the FBI again.

But if Yuuto backed down now, then coming all the way to Los

Angeles would have been for nothing. No—he has to get Rob to talk about Nathan, one way or another.

Yuuto quickly weighed his options and settled on a gamble.

"I was at Schelger Prison not long ago," Yuuto said. "That's where I met Nathan."

"Oh?" Rob tilted his head, curiosity sparking. "What were you, a guard or something?"

Rob asked the question with a hint of amusement in his voice, clearly assuming it wasn't true.

"I wasn't a guard," Yuuto said.

"Then what were you?"

Instead of replying immediately, Yuuto held Rob's gaze.

"I was a prisoner. I was incarcerated in Schelger Prison…as a criminal."

For the first time, real interest flickered in Rob's eyes. He was hooked, at least professionally. Yuuto silently urged him, *Take the bait.* But before Rob could reply, an unexpected interruption broke the tension—a baby's cry echoed from somewhere inside the house.

"Oh, Katie's awake. Hold on a sec—actually, no, come in."

Rob hurriedly gestured for him to enter, and Yuuto followed him into the house. Through an open doorway on the right was a spacious living room.

"What's the matter, Katie? Hungry? Or is it your diaper? Hm?" Rob's voice softened as he picked up the crying baby from the couch. She couldn't have been more than a year old, with a round face and adorable. "Ah, diaper it is. All right, we'll fix that. No more crying, princess."

He pressed several kisses to her chubby cheeks, then grabbed a fresh diaper from a nearby pack. Watching Rob change her with practiced ease, Yuuto couldn't help but remember all the times he and Paco had changed Lupita's diapers together.

"Agent Lennix, right?" Rob said over his shoulder. "Go ahead and sit anywhere."

Yuuto sat down on the sofa across from him. For some reason, Rob then handed Katie over to him.

"Mind watching her for a second? I'll get us some coffee. It's the least I can do."

Yuuto wanted to tell him he didn't need coffee—he needed information—but Rob's tone allowed no room for argument.

Katie looked up at him with wide blue eyes, clearly examining the unfamiliar face holding her. He hadn't held a baby in years, and for a moment, he worried she might start crying. Instead, she suddenly grinned broadly, showing off her tiny new teeth as she laughed loudly.

"What's so funny, huh? Is my face that amusing?" He gently poked her cheek with his finger, earning more giggles.

When Rob returned with two steaming mugs, he paused and grinned. "Well, would you look at that? My little princess is in a good mood. And here I thought she was shy around strangers."

Rob set the two cups on the table, then gently scooped Katie into his arms. With a tender smile, he softly rubbed his nose against her tiny one.

"You really are a little girl, huh?" he teased. "Of course you'd love a handsome guy like this."

"Is your wife out right now?" Yuuto asked.

"I don't have a wife. I'm single," Rob said with a laugh as he sat down on the sofa.

"I see…" Yuuto murmured, glancing away. Maybe his wife had left him. Yuuto couldn't help but feel a twinge of sympathy. Raising a child this young on his own must be incredibly tough. Speaking just to break the silence, Yuuto offered, "It must be tough, taking care of her by yourself."

"Yeah, I still mess up all the time," Rob admitted. "Kids… they're really not easy."

"You're doing a remarkable job, Mr. Connors. It's not something many men could manage on their own."

"You think so? But it's not like I'm raising her full-time," Rob replied. "I only watch Katie two or three times a month."

"What?" Yuuto blinked in confusion.

"She's my niece," Rob explained with a small smile. "My sister lives nearby. Her babysitter canceled at the last minute, so I'm filling in today."

"Oh…"

Realizing his mistake, Yuuto felt his face warm with embarrassment. Katie wasn't Rob's daughter after all. "S-sorry. I jumped to conclusions."

"It's fine. I can't blame you," Rob replied, his eyes glinting mischievously, like a kid who'd just pulled off a harmless prank. He'd probably noticed Yuuto's misunderstanding from the start and let it happen on purpose. It wasn't worth getting angry over, but it still left Yuuto feeling awkward as he brought his cup to his lips.

Rob was happy to talk about minor topics, but when it came to Nathan, he avoided every question with vague answers and playful tricks. No matter how stubbornly Yuuto pressed, Rob's lips stayed closed. Rob finally said, "Sorry, but you could camp out here all night and it still wouldn't change anything."

"I'm not giving up. I *will* find out what I need to know about Nathan," Yuuto answered firmly. "I'll leave for now, but I'll be back tomorrow."

"Tomorrow, I'll be at the university," Rob replied casually. "I'm only part-time, but I go in a few times a month."

"Then…would it be alright if I visited you at the university?" Yuuto asked.

"You don't give up, do you?" Rob sighed and shrugged, as if surrendering to Yuuto's persistence. "Alright, how about I make you a proposal?"

"Go ahead," Yuuto replied.

"I don't want to tell the FBI anything about Nathan," Rob said. "But if it were a trusted friend asking me…I might be willing to talk."

Yuuto looked at Rob's relaxed smile while he comforted Katie, trying to understand his words. "What exactly do you mean by that?"

"I mean, if you can become my friend, I'll help you," Rob explained simply.

Yuuto hesitated. He couldn't quite say, *"Alright, let's be friends from this moment on,"* and then be done with it.

"And how am I supposed to do that?"

"Well," Rob said thoughtfully. "How about this? Let's go to my favorite bar, grab a few drinks, and by the time we leave, I bet we'll be joking around like old pals. What do you say?"

Yuuto almost wondered if Rob was teasing him, but the look in his eyes told him he was completely serious.

"Alright," Yuuto agreed at last. "I'll do it your way."

"That's what I wanted to hear," Rob said, looking satisfied. "My sister will be here soon to pick up Katie. Once she's gone, we'll head out in my car. However, I do have one warning—my regular spot is a little unconventional. You'll just have to put up with it."

Watching Rob's cheerful expression, Yuuto couldn't rid himself of a faint feeling of unease.

CHAPTER 4

While gripping the steering wheel, Rob reintroduced himself:

"I'm thirty-four. I studied at the University of Virginia, then went on to Georgetown in D.C. Three years ago, I came back, and now I'm teaching as a visiting professor at my alma mater, the University of California."

It was an impressive résumé—enough to make Yuuto want to applaud. Being invited back as a visiting professor at that age, Rob must have accumulated a wealth of experience and accomplishments. And yet, Rob's demeanor was relaxed and approachable, with no sign of arrogance. He might have been a little eccentric, but Yuuto found his straightforward attitude refreshing.

"Just call me Rob," he said. "I don't care much for formalities, so let's keep things casual. Deal?"

"Deal. Then call me Yuuto," Yuuto replied.

Rob's SUV rolled into West Hollywood, which sits between Hollywood and Beverly Hills. As they drove down Melrose Avenue, Yuuto noticed many same-sex couples holding hands. Known for its trendy and stylish shops, the area is also famous for its large LGBTQ community—even the city's mayor is openly gay. Every year, West Hollywood hosts one of the biggest Pride parades in the country.

Rob pulled up in front of a building and stopped the car. Apparently, parking was valet service here. He stepped out, handed the keys to an attendant, and turned back to Yuuto with a grin. "Come on. Even though it's a club, most of the crowd here is made up of adults, so it's not too wild. You'll probably like it."

Not too wild, maybe—yet as soon as they stepped inside, pounding dance music almost made Yuuto's ears ache. They found two open seats at the bar, tucked away in the back of the club where the noise wasn't quite as intense. From there, they could actually have a conversation without shouting.

Yuuto glanced around and immediately understood what kind of place Rob had brought him to.

Men.

Everywhere.

A few women were scattered among the crowd, but, as expected, they were wrapped around each other in intimate pairs. Rob had brought him to a gay club.

Rob ordered a non-alcoholic beer. Yuuto blinked in surprise—he'd assumed Rob would be planning to take a cab home if he intended to drink.

"I thought we were drinking the night away," Yuuto said.

"Not tonight," Rob replied. "Don't worry about it. I have a little talent for getting drunk on the atmosphere alone. Go ahead and order whatever you'd like, and I'll make sure you get where you need to go afterward."

Yuuto wasn't sure if Rob was just being polite because he was the one who invited him. Despite his boldness, Rob was surprisingly gentlemanly in unexpected ways. Yuuto still couldn't quite figure him out.

"Hey, Rob!" someone called. A slender young man in a tight, glittery T-shirt waved at him. "Long time no see."

"Hey, Marv. How've you been?" The two greeted each other warmly, hugging before sharing a quick, casual kiss.

"Is this your new boyfriend? If so, I guess you've finally gotten over Al," Marv said, giving Yuuto an appraising look.

"Sorry to disappoint you, but no—" Rob chuckled. "He's not that kind of partner."

"Oh. So he's just a friend, then?"

"Not exactly. We're still in the middle of a test to see if we can be friends," Rob replied with a smirk.

Marv tilted his head in bafflement and muttered, "Ugh. I hate testing people just to decide if you're friends," before wandering off.

Yuuto raised an eyebrow. "If all you wanted to know was whether I'm okay with gay people, you could've just asked me instead of going through this whole song and dance."

"A polite answer doesn't tell you what someone really thinks," Rob said lightly, lifting his glass as if to dismiss Yuuto's complaint. "And for the record, that bit about testing you was a joke. I brought you here because I wanted us to have a good time together. So, not too uncomfortable, I hope?"

Rob's easygoing attitude was strangely disarming. For all Yuuto's initial suspicion, it seemed like maybe Rob really did just want to spend a pleasant evening together—no hidden agenda, no strings attached.

"Don't worry. I don't have any prejudice against gay people," Yuuto said.

For a moment, he even entertained the wicked thought of saying he'd slept with a man before, just to see Rob's reaction—but no, he wasn't about to go that far with someone he'd just met.

"Wanna dance?" Rob asked.

"I'll pass. You go ahead and enjoy yourself."

"No way. I told you, tonight's about getting to know you."

Rob seemed to know half the club; several men approached him to chat, and a few even asked him to dance. But each time, Rob declined with a friendly smile and a promise of "maybe next time."

He was a university professor who navigated gay life with an ease that felt totally natural. Yuuto found himself becoming more curious about Rob himself.

"So, are you a closeted gay man?" Yuuto asked.

"No," Rob replied with a casual grin. "I'm out to the people around me."

Yuuto had already guessed that. Seeing Rob's relaxed warmth and friendly attitude, it's hard to believe he ever had trouble being gay.

As Yuuto sipped his second beer, his thoughts unexpectedly drifted toward his own sexuality. He had slept with Dick. At the time, he hadn't felt even a flicker of disgust. He'd never questioned that he was straight, but maybe he'd just failed to notice a part of himself until now.

"Rob, can I ask you something?" Yuuto said.

"Sure. What is it?"

"Say a guy who's always lived his life straight suddenly ends up having sex with another man, and it doesn't bother him at all. Would you say he's gay?"

Rob's lips curved in quiet amusement at the blunt question.

"There isn't enough information to judge. Why did he do it? Was he pressured into it and lacked the courage to say no? Or… did he want it because he genuinely liked the guy?"

"Probably the latter. He wanted it because he liked him."

"Then yeah, maybe he's gay. But honestly, I think the bigger question isn't whether he's gay or straight. It's whether what he feels for that man is truly love."

"Why?" Yuuto asked, frowning. "I'd think most straight guys in that situation would be scrambling to figure out if they're gay."

"That's pointless," Rob replied with a shrug. "If he can't accept his feelings without first labeling himself, then he's not truly in love with the guy. Not really. Sexuality and emotions don't always align perfectly."

Yuuto let out a sigh. "That's…complicated."

"Seems to me you're the kind of guy who likes to analyze everything," Rob said with a knowing smile. "But love doesn't work that way. When your eyes meet, does your heart skip a beat? When you touch, does your body heat up? When you can't see him, do you miss him? If the answer's yes, then there's your truth."

"That's…almost annoyingly simple," Yuuto admitted with a faint laugh. "I'm gonna hit the restroom."

He pushed himself up, weaving through the crowded floor until he slipped out into the hallway. Inside the restroom, a couple was practically devouring each other against the wall.

Yuuto ignored them and walked to a urinal, but the two of them didn't seem to notice or care about his presence. They were caught up in a tangle of lips and hands, softly moaning as they clung to each other. He had seen plenty of kissing here, but this—this was different. It was raw, unfiltered lust.

As Yuuto was leaving, the younger man pinned against the wall glanced over his partner's shoulder. Their eyes met. His cheeks were flushed, his lips swollen from kissing, but he still managed to flash Yuuto a playful, breathless smile.

"Wanna join us?" the younger man teased with a grin.

"I'll pass," Yuuto replied with a wry smile and slipped back into the hallway.

It made sense. In a place like this—surrounded only by men—it's no surprise everyone was so uninhibited. Everywhere he looked, men were kissing, embracing, and laughing freely, and they all seemed genuinely happy. Their faces were bright and open. Some might call it shameless, maybe even decadent, but the truth was simpler. These men were truly living—*really living*—in this moment.

Yuuto knew he couldn't step into that world. Not because he wasn't gay, but because he lacked the luxury of enjoying life like they did. Still…a small part of him envied them.

He lingered there for a moment, watching the men dance in the glow of neon lights, their movements relaxed and joyful, until finally he returned to Rob, who then drove him back to his hotel. When Rob asked for the name of his hotel, Yuuto told him, and as promised, Rob took the wheel and drove him safely to the underground parking lot.

"Thanks for coming out with me," Rob said with an easy smile.

"Rob…do you think I've got what it takes to be your friend yet?" Yuuto asked.

Rob's smile flickered. He hesitated for a moment, then let out a soft, almost apologetic sigh.

"About that…I don't think I can."

The disappointment hit Yuuto harder than he had expected. They'd laughed together, shared drinks, and talked like they'd known each other for years. For a moment, he truly believed he'd broken down Rob's walls—believed Rob might finally tell him what he knew about Nathan.

"What didn't you like about me?" Yuuto pressed, unable to hide the urgency in his voice. Time was running out. If he didn't get new information by the day after tomorrow, he'd have to leave L.A.

"Yuuto, I like you a lot." Rob chuckled softly, almost helplessly. "You're serious, polite, and honestly, I don't have a single complaint."

"Then why?" Yuuto demanded. "If there's no problem, why can't we be friends?"

Rob's expression softened. He looked at Yuuto for a long moment, then reached out, lightly brushing his fingertips against

Yuuto's cheek.

"If I had to give you an answer," Rob murmured, smiling faintly. "It's that I like you too much. You're…too good to just be a friend."

The touch was gentle, almost tender, and at that moment, Yuuto finally understood what Rob meant.

"Rob," Yuuto said firmly, catching his hand and pulling it away. "I'm sorry. But I'm not interested in that."

"I know," Rob replied with an easy shrug. "I just wanted to be honest about how I feel."

A heavy silence filled the car. Yuuto exhaled heavily, feeling trapped from all sides. "So, what? Was this all just a joke to you?"

"No," Rob replied calmly. "I really did want to be your friend. This…this is just an accident."

"You're unbelievable," Yuuto muttered, shooting him a sharp glare. "What's your game here, Rob? What do you actually want from me?"

If Rob was openly hinting at his ulterior motives, then it was clear—he had to be planning to trade Nathan's information for something inappropriate.

"Thanks for asking," Rob said lightly, almost relieved. "Alright, I'll be straight with you. Yuuto, let me kiss you."

CHAPTER 5

Yuuto slumped back in his seat, feeling completely caught off guard by how cheerful and straightforward the man was. "What kind of man *are* you? I can't tell if you're a good guy or a total trainwreck."

Rob chuckled. "I don't know either. Honestly, I'm kind of impressed with myself right now. I didn't think I was the type to pull this kind of stunt…and yet, here we are."

Under normal circumstances, Yuuto would have been furious—he would have looked at Rob with disgust. But the man's unshakable, almost absurdly easygoing demeanor left him more exasperated than angry. He wasn't even hateable. Taking him seriously felt almost laughable.

"Just a kiss? That's all? And if I let you, you'll tell me what you know about Nathan?"

Yuuto's tone was flat, resigned. Maybe it was the exhaustion, or maybe he'd just stopped caring, but if one kiss was the price for a crucial lead, then so be it.

"Yeah," Rob promised. "I swear. I might be a lot of things, but I'm not the kind of bastard who'd force someone into bed against their will."

"Fine. Do what you want." Yuuto faced forward, his expression stony.

Rob grinned, leaned over, and with a breezy "Excuse me," abruptly reclined Yuuto's seat all the way back.

"That's completely unnecessary!" Yuuto snapped.

"Oh, come on," Rob said with a teasing lilt. "If we're gonna do this, might as well set the mood."

Rob leaned over him, and Yuuto shot him a glacial look in return.

"You know," Rob murmured, amused. "I'm not a masochist, but when you look at me like that… It's kind of hot."

"Rob. Stop talking. Just get it over with already," Yuuto said icily.

"Yeah, yeah. Hold still." Rob only laughed under his breath. "Please don't bite my tongue off. I'm not trying to bleed to death here."

"If I do anything beyond a kiss, I can't guarantee what'll happen." Desperate to get it over with, Yuuto closed his eyes and braced himself. But no matter how long he waited, Rob's lips never touched him.

Peering through half-closed eyes, he watched Rob struggling to hold back his laughter right in front of him. "Rob?"

"You're adorable," Rob said, barely containing his grin. "Taking my joke seriously like that."

A joke.

That one word made Yuuto's mind go completely blank. "Were you teasing me?"

"Sorry. I honestly thought you'd flat-out refuse the kiss."

Yuuto's cheeks flushed with a blend of embarrassment and frustration. He was left speechless. Gathering all his strength, he shoved Rob away forcefully. "Move."

Rob yelped and collapsed back into the driver's seat.

"You're the worst. Is my desperation really that funny to you?" Yuuto stormed out of the car.

"Yuuto, wait—" Rob started to say, but Yuuto ignored him and slammed the door shut hard. Almost right away, Rob rolled down the passenger window and leaned out. "I am sorry for teasing you. Please wait!"

Without looking back, Yuuto kept walking, but Rob shouted after him, "Tomorrow at 3 o'clock! Come to my place."

Yuuto halted and spun around, a fierce scowl on his face. "Why?"

"I'll talk about Nathan. I promise. I'll tell you everything I know." Rob's expression was completely serious.

"Can I trust you?"

"Yeah. I apologize for acting disrespectfully while you were really working. I genuinely regret it. So please, trust me."

Hearing Rob's desperate plea, Yuuto could only respond, "Alright. I'll definitely come tomorrow."

"Good," Rob said. "I'll be waiting. Good night."

Once inside his hotel room, Yuuto headed straight for the shower. After spending so long at the club, the smell of alcohol and cigarettes clung to his body. Fresh and clean, he slipped naked beneath the sheets, drained in a way he hadn't expected. Rob had completely thrown him around. At times like this, the best thing was to stop thinking and just sleep.

Though still irritated, Yuuto comforted himself with the thought that tomorrow he would finally hear about Nathan. It hadn't been a wasted effort.

Tomorrow, *it would be different*, he promised himself.

But even with his eyes closed, sleep didn't come easily. Tossing and turning in frustration, images from the club—intense scenes of men in passionate embraces—and Rob's face after they parted kept flashing through his mind.

If Rob had been serious, Yuuto thought, he would have kissed that man in the car. Suddenly, imagining that possibility made him quickly push the thought away. It wasn't that he wanted to kiss him.

Definitely not.

Still, he felt restless and unsettled. Maybe it was frustration. He realized he hadn't masturbated in several days. Maybe if he took care of himself, he'd feel clearer and fall asleep.

Reluctantly, he reached down and started to stimulate himself. He thought he could just go through the motions, but scattered fantasies raced wildly through his mind.

The passionate scenes of men at the club somehow shifted their focus to him and Dick, with yearning and heated touches. In the infirmary shower room, Dick had comforted him with his hands. Remembering that moment, his strokes quickened.

Dick was touching him. Imagining it, his arousal only grew stronger.

Dick…Dick, just—

"What do you want? You're feeling it so much." The whisper from long ago echoed in his ears, a sweet ache stirring deep in his chest.

Dick. Dick. I want to see you. I want to see you right now.

"Mm…"

Just as he was about to give in to the strong pleasure, another voice echoed in his mind.

"Hey, BB, how's that little yellow bitch's hole?"

"Tight…Fuckin' perfect."

Yuuto's entire body stiffened. The blood drained from his face, and nausea surged within him. Naturally, the arousal disappeared instantly, and he couldn't go on.

"Damn…" he spat the words weakly and buried his head in his hands on the bed.

The horrible memories from the prison shower room sometimes surfaced unexpectedly like this. Especially when he remembered the sex with Dick, those dark images flooded back as well.

Since his last HIV test was negative, he felt much lighter mentally. However, the fear of illness and the trauma of being raped were two separate burdens. The wounds in his heart did not heal easily. He knew that forgetting was the best approach—to forget everything and erase it all.

Yuuto pulled the sheets over his head and waited desperately for sleep to come.

CHAPTER 6

The next day, before heading to Rob's house, Yuuto contacted the FBI's Los Angeles office. He requested to speak with an agent named Jefferson, who had been recommended by Heiden, to learn more about what kind of man Rob Connors was.

"Rob Connors?" Jeff pondered. "Oh, that guy. He's still young but a great scholar. A bit of an oddball, but someone you can rely on. If I remember right, last year's string of murders in Burbank was solved thanks to Connors's help. The suspect was caught because of him."

"He said he's no longer willing to cooperate with the FBI. I wonder what happened," Yuuto said.

Jefferson fell silent for a moment. "I think I know why," he muttered. "During the Burbank case, Connors used profiling to narrow down the suspect, but the FBI dismissed his opinion, claiming it didn't match the evidence left at the scene. In the end, Connors was right, but because of the FBI's stubbornness, it took longer to find the killer, and more victims died. Connors was furious and reportedly said the FBI should just disappear for the sake of society—or something like that."

Yuuto couldn't imagine the mild-mannered Rob getting that angry, but it had to be serious. Not because his opinion was ignored, but because the FBI's negligence had cost more lives.

Although Rob's behavior—using information as bait to demand a kiss and then laughing it off as a joke—was the lowest, Yuuto didn't think he was a bad person. He believed that Rob would probably share some details of the investigation and be willing to cooperate.

As promised, Yuuto arrived at Rob's house at three o'clock.

"Hey, Yuuto. Glad you came," Rob greeted him with a fresh smile, giving no hint of yesterday's events. "Did you sleep well last night?"

"Thanks to you, I slept soundly until morning," Yuuto replied curtly, sitting down on the sofa.

"Are you still mad?" Rob asked, looking troubled.

"I'm mad. I'm not the kind of person who can smile after being lectured and pressured into a kiss as a joke," Yuuto said.

Rob sat across from him, frowning as if genuinely surprised. "Yeah, the kiss thing was a joke. But it's true that I like you. I'm seriously attracted to you. If possible, I want something more than just friendship."

Rob took this chance to say sweet things, but Yuuto didn't even smile.

"Rob, I want to be upfront with you. Please don't give me that kind of look. I think we can be friends, but nothing more."

"Is that so? Depending on how hard I try, you might just change your mind," Rob said with an infuriating smile. "Life's unpredictable. Don't decide things from the start—let's just take it easy."

"You're annoyingly optimistic." Yuuto shook his head.

"Yeah. Positive thinking is my greatest virtue."

"Tell me about Nathan, like we agreed." Yuuto shifted his mood and got down to business.

"Wait a minute." Rob held out his hand and stopped him. "I'll tell you everything I know. But before we talk about Nathan, can you tell me about your background? Yesterday, you said some strange things… about being a prisoner."

That story was something Yuuto mentioned yesterday to try to catch Rob's interest. He thought it didn't work, but apparently Rob remembered it well.

"I want to learn more about you. I've never heard of an ex-convict becoming an FBI agent. One of the requirements for investigators is having a clean moral record. So how did someone with a serious criminal background like yours pass the exam?"

Trusting Rob, Yuuto briefly explained his past: he was a DEA agent, was wrongfully imprisoned, and after his release, was recruited by the FBI as an investigator.

Rob didn't seem convinced by the patchy explanation, and when Yuuto finished, he came at him with sharp questions.

"There are too many strange parts in your story," he said. "Why were you transferred from New York to California? And even though the real culprit in your colleague's murder was identified with solid evidence and confessed, the quick acquittal after the retrial seems suspicious. Also, why would the FBI recruit someone like you with a complicated background?"

Rob's face grew stern. When the smile disappeared, his sharp intellect became clear. "Sorry, but I'm not here to listen to half-baked stories. If you're telling the truth, then tell it straight—don't leave anything out."

It seemed Yuuto wouldn't hear anything about Nathan until he told the whole truth. He steeled himself.

"Alright. I'll tell you everything, but I want you to promise that what you're about to hear stays between us."

Rob nodded immediately. "I promise. Whatever you say, I'll keep it a secret. I'd even sign a confidentiality agreement if you want."

"No need. I trust you."

Yuuto couldn't separate his background from the Nathan case. If he tried to evade the truth, he'd only make things worse for himself. So he spoke honestly, filling in every detail he had previously left vague.

Everything. From the link between the bombings across the United States and the mysterious cult group. To the existence of Corvus, who had been undercover in prison as Nathan, and how Corvus exploited the chaos during a riot, escaping with the help of the prison warden.

"The warden was found dead. Most likely the work of Corvus."

By the time Yuuto finished, Rob's expression had darkened further, more grave than before. A chill of worry passed through him—was his story so implausible that it had only deepened Rob's doubt?

"Rob, it's not a lie. Please believe me. I'm desperate to find Corvus. Please, tell me what you know about Nathan."

Yuuto's plea appeared to bring Rob back to himself. His expression softened.

"I'm not doubting you. It's fascinating—well, no, I mean… interesting stuff."

Yuuto pulled a photo borrowed from the Los Angeles Police Department out of his suit's inner pocket and handed it over. "This is a photo of Nathan from his arrest. Look closely—do you think it's really him? Doesn't he look like someone who's had surgery to resemble him?"

Rob examined the photo for a long moment.

"Hmm," he muttered. "Now that you mention it, something does look different. Honestly, I only met Nathan face-to-face three times, so I can't swear to it from one picture. Still, I believe your story. Nathan wasn't the one in charge—he was just taking orders."

Yuuto was surprised by this sudden insight.

"What kind of relationship did you have with Nathan?" he pressed. "Now it's your turn."

Finally, onto the real topic. It made Yuuto tense up, waiting for

Rob's words.

"Wait here a moment," Rob said and left the living room. After a while, he returned carrying a laptop. "I'm going to show you some footage of Nathan. It was recorded during an interview with him."

"Interview?"

"Let me start from the beginning. Six months before Nathan's arrest for killing his mother, I gave a lecture on mind control and brainwashing." Rob paused in his retelling. "Right—I should add that I study psychology. In that talk, I broke down for the general public how behavior, thoughts, and emotions can be twisted and reshaped, using real cases from cults and crimes as examples."

Yuuto listened intently, determined not to miss a single word.

"By coincidence, Nathan also came to hear that lecture. Later, he called the university lab and explained he was part of a certain cult group. Nathan thought what he was doing might be wrong, but he couldn't leave the organization, and asked for advice on what to do."

Yuuto clenched his fists instinctively. That cult group had to be White Heaven. Nathan was clearly one of Corvus's followers. Realizing this made the trip to L.A. worthwhile.

"I was very interested, so I decided to meet him. After meeting twice and breaking the ice a little, I invited him to my house for an interview. I had to convince him that I would never report him to the police and that it was just for my research… Alright, I'll play it now."

Rob tapped some keys and launched the video player. Soon, the footage appeared.

"What's your name?" Rob's voice, off-camera, asked the question.

The man sitting nervously on the sofa answered, *"Nathan. Nathan Clark."*

"That's Nathan. Not the same guy who was in prison, right?" Rob asked.

"Yeah," Yuuto nodded firmly. "They look alike, but they're different people. Their builds and voices don't match."

"What's the name of your organization?"

"White Heaven... Hey, please don't tell anyone. If they find out what I said, they'll kill me." Nathan's eyes were full of fear. Yuuto could tell he was genuinely terrified.

"Don't worry, you're safe. What kind of organization is White Heaven? Does it have any religious teachings?"

"It's not a religion. It's an ideological group. We're volunteers committed to reforming society, even if it requires using force, based on the teachings of a great leader, fighting against corrupt politics and capitalist society—"

Nathan kept talking and talking, almost like he was reading from a textbook, explaining the organization's structure and goals. But to Yuuto, it just sounded like a bunch of antisocial people making selfish excuses to vent their frustrations through cowardly acts of terror.

"How can anyone be brainwashed by an ideology like this?" Yuuto asked, brow furrowed in disbelief.

Rob grinned. "It's easier than you think. Just wait until you hear the rest of Nathan's story. 'Outrageous' doesn't even begin to cover this group."

As Yuuto folded his arms and sank into thought, Rob rose to his feet.

"Let's take a break. I'll make some coffee."

Left alone, Yuuto exhaled deeply and leaned back against the sofa.

CHAPTER 7

The actual interview with Nathan lasted nearly an hour. To be honest, it was a huge success. For the first time, they gathered a lot of information about White Heaven, an organization that had been nothing more than a shadow until now.

White Heaven's main source of income was drugs. Nathan had confessed that, under the organization's orders, he'd been involved in cocaine trafficking. His role was that of a courier, transporting large shipments of cocaine smuggled through Mexico all the way to Los Angeles.

They also discovered that most of White Heaven's founding members had graduated from the Military School for Security Cooperation, also known as MSC. According to Nathan's testimony, even Corvus himself had attended there.

MSC was a military training camp in Texas. Although it was said to be legally operated with government approval, Yuuto didn't really understand what happened inside. Maybe it was because so much information had hit him all at once, but his thoughts were scattered. He needed Rob, the expert, to help him organize everything.

Rob returned with fresh coffee. Yuuto thanked him and accepted a cup.

"What's with the long face? Nathan's story wasn't helpful?"

"Of course it was. I never imagined I'd get information this valuable. I'm just…having trouble keeping up. About MSC—I haven't heard many good things. What's their actual purpose?"

"Officially, they're an aid organization dedicated to peace and human rights," Rob explained. "All it takes is tuition and a basic screening, and you're in. They boast about training law enforcement and disaster-relief teams, but the truth? It's a breeding ground for terrorists."

Yuuto had heard similar rumors before. Many former MSC graduates from Central and South America had become infamous dictators or state-sponsored terrorists.

"The truth is that the camp's funded by the government," Rob continued. "It was originally established during the Cold War, under the pretense of eradicating leftist guerrillas in Central and South America. The U.S. government created it to strengthen foreign militaries. Its real goal was to halt the spread of socialism in the region and keep it under control. It's basically a relic of darker history. White Heaven might even have some kind of connection to the government."

Yuuto shook his head. "I don't think so."

"What makes you so sure?"

"I didn't mention this earlier," Yuuto said, hesitating briefly before adding, "The CIA is trying to assassinate Corvus. If he had government ties, that wouldn't make any sense, would it?"

"What? The CIA is involved in this too?"

Earlier, Yuuto deliberately avoided mentioning the CIA because he didn't want to bring up Dick.

"Yeah. There was a CIA agent in Schelger Prison who was after Corvus," Yuuto said. "He went by the alias Dick. Like me, he'd been planted there as a prisoner. Dick was a former Army soldier—during the White Heaven siege, Corvus killed his comrades. So he took a mission from the CIA to assassinate Corvus as revenge. That's how he ended up in Schelger. He kept an eye on me, thinking I was FBI, but when the riot broke out, he escaped, chasing after Corvus."

"You really are like a jack-in-the-box, Yuuto." Rob let out a long, exasperated sigh and ran his fingers through his hair. "One surprise after another."

"Sorry. I couldn't explain everything all at once."

"It's fine." Rob waved it off casually. "I'm an outsider, and we just met. It's natural for there to be things you couldn't say right away. Now, let's get back to Nathan and White Heaven. From that interview—what else stood out to you?"

"Well…the part about White Heaven dealing drugs. It's just as strange as the bombings. The members probably joined because they believed in these grand ideals, but how do they not see the contradiction in what they're doing?"

"Nathan kept justifying himself by saying the U.S. government was the one that first spread cocaine," Rob explained. "And honestly, from a historical perspective, he might not be entirely wrong. There were times when the government looked the other way—or even had a hand in it—because of political motives. That kind of narrative gives them a psychological escape route: if the government did it too, then it can't be that wrong."

"Plus, it seems like White Heaven's members received a lot of money to support their 'activities.' Corvus is clever. He probably attracts them with ideology first, then offers money to weaken their judgment."

Rob explained that most people who entered cult-like groups had already abandoned their families, their work, and their friends. To later admit they had chosen wrongly was a psychological burden too heavy to bear.

To avoid that, they turned away from reality, clung to self-justification, and eventually, their faith hardened into fanaticism—until they were capable of outrageous acts.

"In psychology, we call it cognitive dissonance theory," Rob went on. "When people do something they know is wrong, they don't change their actions—they change how they see it. That's easier, right? They cherry-pick whatever information makes them feel better. But Nathan… he was starting to want change. Deprogramming methods for cults aren't well-developed yet, so I thought helping him might also teach me something…"

"When was the last time you saw him?" Yuuto asked.

"The last time I saw him was during that interview. Afterward, I couldn't reach him. All I had was his cell phone number… Then, a few months later, I saw the news—Nathan had killed his mother. I went to the LAPD, but they wouldn't let me see him. After that, I didn't know where he'd been sent. I blamed myself for not saving him, but…deep down, I told myself maybe it was better this way. At least he was free from the organization. Classic cognitive dissonance, huh?"

Rob shrugged, but Yuuto stayed silent. For Rob, Nathan was a painful memory he preferred not to recall.

"But if the person who was arrested was a fake," Rob said. "Then what happened to the real Nathan?"

"Just speculation," Yuuto began cautiously. "But…worst case, Corvus might have already killed him."

Rob fell silent, clearly disturbed by the idea. "So Corvus killed Nathan's mother?"

"That's what I think. By the time of the arrest, he had already undergone plastic surgery. It had to be part of a well-planned scheme." Yuuto explained his theory to Rob.

After the siege incident, Corvus must have realized the danger of his situation. So, he came up with the idea of hiding inside a prison by using someone else's identity. He selected Nathan from his followers. Nathan had no criminal record, and his build and hair color were a good match. He was the ideal candidate.

After the surgery was over, Corvus killed Nathan and then murdered his only close family member—his mother. All he had to do next was turn himself in and be sent to prison as Nathan.

"Sounds about right," Rob said with a grim nod. "But even if we know that, it doesn't tell us where Corvus is now. So, what's your next move?"

"I'm going to Schelger Prison," Yuuto said. "There's someone there I need to talk to. After that, I'll trace Nathan's cocaine trail. If I can find White Heaven members, I can get closer to Corvus. Rob, do you know anything about the gang Nathan worked with in the drug trade?"

"He mentioned a Chicano gang. I believe it was called *Ara Roja*. The police might have more information about them."

"Then I'll ask my brother. He's a detective with the LAPD."

Rob looked at Yuuto in surprise. "Your brother's a detective, too? Impressive family."

"He's my stepbrother. We're not related by blood. He's Chicano."

"Huh. What about you, Yuuto? Chinese? Korean?"

"Neither. I'm Japanese."

They talked for a while about their backgrounds and families until Rob asked if Yuuto was planning to visit Schelger Prison the next day. When Yuuto said yes, Rob surprised him again by asking if he could come along as well.

"I won't get in the way of your investigation. Just let me come along. I've always wanted to visit that prison." Rob looked at Yuuto with an unexpectedly cheerful expression, waiting for his answer. Despite being such a well-structured adult, he sometimes revealed a strange, almost childlike side.

Yuuto couldn't help but chuckle. "Research, huh?"

"A very useful bit of fieldwork," Rob replied quickly. "I also study prison systems. When it comes to understanding the justice and correctional systems, prisons are incredibly symbolic places.

Privatization, the reality of the corrections industry—there's so much to explore. What? Why are you looking at me like that?"

Before Yuuto realized it, he'd reached out and grabbed Rob's hand. "Y-Yuuto?" Rob blinked in surprise. "What's wrong?"

"Amazing. You're the real jack-in-the-box here, Rob."

Before Dick escaped, he mentioned that a crucial clue was hidden in Corvus's comments about the prison system. It was so vague that Yuuto didn't know what to make of it. But if anyone could help him understand it, it would be Rob—with his deep knowledge of prison operations.

"Coming to L.A. and meeting you has been the best thing that's happened to me," Yuuto admitted.

Rob gave a small, almost bashful smile. "I'm glad to hear that."

"If you're willing, could I ask you to assist with the investigation officially? As long as I'm in town, I'd really like to be able to consult with you." Yuuto half-expected Rob to refuse. After all, Rob had said before that he didn't want to work with the FBI anymore. But letting someone this capable slip away wasn't an option.

"Sure. I'll help you."

Yuuto blinked. "Seriously?"

"Of course. This case is too fascinating to pass up. And besides, there's Nathan. I want to know what happened to him, even if he's nothing more than a corpse now."

Yuuto extended his hand for a proper handshake, and Rob firmly gripped it.

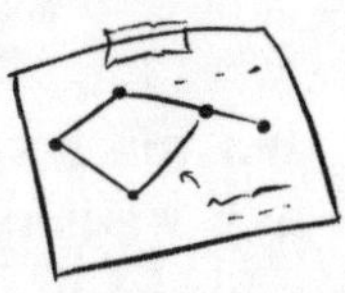

"This is Schelger Prison?" Rob said from behind the wheel, his voice filled with awe. “It’s huge.”

Sitting in the passenger seat, Yuuto looked out at the endless line of fencing. A strange mix of feelings surfaced inside him—part familiarity, part dread, and something else he couldn’t quite identify.

The first time he came here, it was on a prison transport bus, peering through the wire-meshed windows. Matthew sat beside him. He remembered the brutal welcome on his first day inside: the beatings, constant racial slurs, disgusting food, and filthy living conditions. Then there was the solitary confinement that nearly drove him mad.

But nothing had affected him as deeply as what happened with BB—the Black gang’s number two.

Yuuto clenched his fists at the memory. In the showers, they held him down. BB had taken him from behind, violently and without mercy. He hadn’t even been able to fight back.

That was the moment when the last thread of his endurance gave way. Until then, Yuuto had borne everything, sustained by the fragile conviction that if he refused to yield, he might survive. But the shattering of his dignity—far more than the breaking of his body—had nearly destroyed him.

And then…there was Dick.

Dick had held him when Yuuto had been ready to fall apart. He hadn’t told him to be strong. Instead, he kissed Yuuto’s forehead and whispered, “It’s okay to fall apart sometimes.”

“Hey. We’re here.” Rob’s voice pulled him out of the memory. Yuuto blinked and saw that the car was already parked. “Let’s go.”

“Yeah…”

He opened the door, but his body fought back, heavy with reluctance. Every part of him wanted to stay in the car. His mind might have been ready, but his body still remembered.

And it hated this place.

"Yuuto. You okay?" Rob had come around to the passenger side, one arm casually braced against the car as he looked down at him with concern.

"I'm fine," Yuuto said, forcing himself to move. He pushed himself up from the seat, his legs stiff but steady.

"If you're not feeling well, we can wait a bit," Rob offered.

"No. I'm fine. Let's go." He patted Rob lightly on the shoulder and started walking.

Yes, Schelger Prison was hell. But hell or not, not everything he'd taken from this place had been worthless. There were no good memories here, but there were things he'd gained.

"By the way," Yuuto said as they neared the entrance. "I'm going to introduce you to the prison staff as FBI. That's okay with you?"

If they discover that Rob lacks the authority to investigate, they might not let him in.

"That's fine…" Rob said with a shrug. "The real question is whether I even look like an FBI agent."

"You'll be fine," Yuuto replied, glancing back at him.

Today, Rob was sharply dressed in a well-fitted suit, his hair perfectly groomed. He looked so different from when they first met that Yuuto almost mistook him for someone else. According to Rob, this was his "real self," and, seeing him like this, Yuuto had to admit that no one would doubt him if he claimed to be an FBI agent.

"By the way, is your brother always like that?" Rob asked.

"Paco? What do you mean, 'like that'?"

"He looked at me like I was a murder suspect. I don't think I made a good first impression."

"It's not that." Yuuto chuckled, recalling the scene from that morning. "He was just worried. I told him I was heading out of town with someone he'd never met, and Paco's always been protective. Normally, he's much friendlier."

The night before, Yuuto told Paco about Rob over dinner. Paco asked question after question until he was sure Rob wasn't some dangerous stranger. Even then, when Rob came to the LAPD station to pick Yuuto up, Paco kept a hawk's eye on him.

"Sorry if it made things awkward," Yuuto added. "Paco's always been like that—maybe even more so since I was falsely accused. He's just…cautious."

Rob smiled. "Sounds like a good brother. But if he's so close to you, why aren't you staying at his place?"

"He offered. But he just moved in with his girlfriend, and I didn't want to intrude."

Paco had called him stubborn for refusing, but Yuuto had booked a hotel anyway. The truth was, Paco's girlfriend made him uncomfortable. She was beautiful, smart, and polite, but the last time Yuuto had stayed over, he'd seen it in her eyes, behind the smile: she wanted him gone.

"Then why don't you stay at my place instead?" Rob offered casually. "I've got a spare room, two cars, and you can borrow one if you want."

Yuuto frowned. "Are you this generous with everyone?"

"Not a chance. Just with certain people," Rob said with a wink.

"Yeah, right." Yuuto rolled his eyes and ignored it. "You've probably got an ulterior motive."

"No, no! Well…" Rob said, then smirked. "Alright, you got me. I do have ulterior motives."

"So which is it—no or yes?" Yuuto said with a wry smile.

"I'm inviting you over because I'm fascinated by this case," Rob explained with a shrug. "That's the scholar in me. As for my personal motives? Those are on hold for now. I'd never push you into anything you don't want, so relax."

"Somehow, that doesn't make me feel any better. You're a devious man, Rob."

Rob only grinned.

Their banter carried them all the way to the prison's central building. At the reception desk, Yuuto introduced himself as an FBI agent and requested a meeting with the warden. They were quickly led into the warden's office, where they met Carter—the new warden.

Carter was a lean man in his early fifties, much more approachable than his predecessor, Corning. He greeted them with a firm handshake and a friendly smile before inviting them to sit.

"Let me guess," Carter said once they were seated. "You're here about Corning's murder, right? I was stunned when I heard. Never thought he'd…"

His voice trailed away as he shook his head.

"Did you know him well?" Yuuto asked.

"Only as a colleague," Carter replied. "Before I was assigned here, I ran a prison in Utah. We crossed paths a few times at company functions and exchanged pleasantries. That was about it."

Schelger Prison was state-owned but privately operated by the Smith-Bucks Company, the largest corrections corporation in the United States, which managed dozens of facilities nationwide.

"When did you transfer here?" Yuuto asked.

"Two weeks ago."

"I see. Well, actually, we're not here about Corning's murder," Yuuto clarified. "We're investigating Nathan Clark. He escaped during the recent riot."

"Ah. Nathan Clark." Carter frowned. "But even if you search the prison, I doubt you'll find anything that will tell you where he went."

"Even the smallest lead would help. I'd like permission to speak with guards and inmates."

Carter hesitated for a moment but finally nodded. "All right. I'll allow it."

Yuuto requested that Captain Guthrie, the head of security, serve as their escort. Carter raised an eyebrow at the specific request but still picked up the phone and called him in.

Five minutes later, Guthrie arrived. He was the officer in charge of the West Wing's A Block—the same unit where Yuuto had once been held. Guthrie's eyes briefly widened in shock at the sight of him, but when Carter introduced Yuuto as FBI, he quickly masked his reaction and returned to a neutral expression.

As they left the warden's office and walked down the central corridor, Yuuto caught up to Guthrie and spoke quietly to him.

"It's been a while, Guthrie," Yuuto said.

"Yeah. What the hell is going on? You were an inmate here not long ago, and now you're FBI?"

"You already knew, didn't you? Dick must've told you."

Yuuto's voice was calm but edged with certainty. The CIA and Dick had suspected him of being an FBI agent, and if Guthrie was working with the CIA, there was a good chance he'd known as well.

"I don't know what you're talking about," Guthrie said flatly.

Yuuto requested a private room, and after a brief pause, Guthrie reluctantly guided them to one of the visitation rooms.

"You helped Dick. You knew what he was here for, didn't you?" Yuuto pressed.

"I have no idea what you're talking about."

"Don't play dumb. I know you're a CIA asset."

Guthrie gave a short, incredulous laugh. "A CIA asset? Me?

Don't be ridiculous."

He wasn't going to admit it. Yuuto was just starting to think about his next move when Rob, who had been silently watching, leaned in closer and whispered, "Don't bother."

Yuuto glanced at him, and Rob added, "Short of torture, he's not going to talk. CIA assets are trained to keep their mouths shut. If they spill even a single secret, they know the Agency might take them out themselves…isn't that right?"

Guthrie glared at Rob, silent but seething.

Yuuto shifted tactics. "Fine. I won't ask whether you worked with the CIA. I would like you to respond as the head of security. This is the kind of information any guard in your position should know."

"What do you want to know?" Guthrie grumbled, after letting out a long, resigned sigh.

"Warden Corning and Nathan Clark," Yuuto said. "They were seen talking privately several times. What was their relationship? Did they know each other before Nathan was brought in?"

Guthrie took off his cap and ran a hand through his hair in frustration. "I don't know the full story. But when Nathan first arrived, Warden Corning told me, *'He's the son of an old friend of mine. Keep an eye out for him.'*"

"And you actually believed that?" Yuuto asked.

"Hell no," Guthrie said, shaking his head. "It was obviously just an excuse. Corning hated Nathan and couldn't stand him. Yet, for some reason, he still treated him like he was untouchable—like he was scared of him. I figured Nathan must've had something on him. Something serious."

Was Corning truly being blackmailed by Nathan? Is that the reason he obeyed him…even helped him escape? It was possible, but something about it didn't sit right with Yuuto.

"Guthrie," Yuuto asked, narrowing his eyes. "Did you know

Nathan was an impostor?"

"What? An impostor? What the hell are you talking about?"

The genuine confusion on Guthrie's face told Yuuto everything he needed to know—he didn't have the whole picture. Of course, the CIA wouldn't share classified information with someone as low-level as a prison contact. Guthrie was probably just following instructions, helping Dick because the Agency told him to.

"Never mind," Yuuto said, letting it drop. "Still, we both know there were guards here who profited from the inmates' gambling rings…or pocketed bribes."

"I wasn't one of them," Guthrie said sharply.

"I know." Yuuto nodded. "You were a good officer, I'll give you that. But those guys existed, didn't they? And if Corning had really wanted Nathan out of the way, he could've used his authority to throw him in solitary—or worse."

"Yeah," Guthrie admitted reluctantly. "That wouldn't have been hard."

"Exactly. Even if Nathan had leverage over him, Corning still possessed the power to cut him off from the outside world. So why didn't he? Why give in so easily?"

Rob, who'd been silent until now, spoke up. "What if it wasn't Nathan himself Corning feared," he said evenly, "but what was behind him?"

Yuuto turned to look at him, and the realization hit. Maybe Corning knew about White Heaven. Maybe he was terrified that crossing Nathan would cause the organization to go beyond the prison walls and eliminate him.

"Is Dr. Spencer still here?" Yuuto asked suddenly.

Spencer, the part-time prison doctor, was also a CIA collaborator—just like Guthrie. Dick had worked in the infirmary as a medical assistant, and if Yuuto was right, Spencer had been his main point of contact with the Agency.

“Yeah,” Guthrie said. “Want me to call him?”

“No,” Yuuto replied. “We’ll go to him. Take us to the infirmary.”

CHAPTER 8

They stepped back out into the corridor. As they walked, Rob kept glancing around, clearly fascinated by the prison's atmosphere. Guthrie shot him an exasperated look.

"Hey, cut it out," Guthrie admonished. "Don't stare at the inmates like that. They're touchier than you think. One wrong look could set something off, and the last thing I need is trouble on my shift."

"Understood," Rob said with a grin. With an almost theatrical flourish, he drew a pair of black sunglasses from his breast pocket and slid them on. Smirking behind the lenses, he added, "This way, they won't even know I'm looking."

Guthrie simply shook his head as if he'd given up.

"Guthrie," Yuuto asked. "Has anything happened here since I left?"

"Lots of small stuff. Fights, smuggling—you know the drill. But nothing major lately… Oh yeah. Rivera got out last week. You were close with him, weren't you?"

"Rivera? He's out?"

Ernesto Rivera—"Neto" to his friends—was the charismatic leader of the Chicano gang *Locos Hermanos*, a man who commanded loyalty from half the prison yard. Yuuto first met him in solitary confinement, of all places, their cells side by side. They bonded without even seeing each other's faces, exchanging words through steel and concrete. After their release from solitary, Neto looked out for Yuuto like a brother.

Yuuto had hoped to catch up with him someday, maybe even thank him face-to-face. But if Neto was free now… Well, Yuuto was glad for him.

When they reached the infirmary, the waiting room was empty—the morning hours had already passed. Yuuto asked Guthrie to wait outside and went in with Rob. Inside, Dr. Spencer sat at his cluttered desk, scribbling something down. His messy hair and scruffy beard hadn't changed at all.

When he looked up and saw Yuuto, his face lit up with genuine surprise.

"Well, well. Yuuto. What's this?" he said in an amused tone. "Are you sick again? Too bad—clinic hours are over."

"Guess I'll just have to come back for that IV later," Yuuto said with a small smile, extending his hand.

Spencer chuckled and shook it firmly. "Good to see you."

"And you, Doctor. You look the same."

Spencer glanced past him, noticing Rob. "And who's this?"

Rob slid his sunglasses off, face perfectly composed. "Agent Connors. FBI."

Yuuto showed his badge, and Spencer blinked at them in disbelief. "You? FBI?"

The shock in his voice didn't sound fake. Yuuto couldn't tell if Spencer was a clever liar or genuinely caught off guard.

"I'm looking for Nathan Clark," Yuuto said.

"The escapee, huh? What about Dick? He broke out, too." Spencer asked casually, but there was a sharpness underneath—the silent test.

"Dick's the LAPD's problem," Yuuto responded calmly. "We're pursuing Nathan because there's reason to suspect he's connected to a criminal organization. You knew Nathan and Dick were close. Did Dick ever mention anything about him?"

Yuuto never expected Spencer to fold at the mention of the CIA. Men like him were built not to. So he framed it as a simple request, as if he were talking to an ordinary prison doctor. Maybe then Spencer would ease up—just enough to slip.

"Sorry, can't help you," Spencer said, leaning back in his chair. "You know Dick—he wasn't exactly the talkative type. The only time he ever ran his mouth was when he was complaining to me."

Yuuto realized there was no use pressing further. If Guthrie had been tight-lipped, Spencer was a vault.

"I see," Yuuto said as he rose. "Well…thank you for your time, Doctor."

"Don't mention it. And for what it's worth…" Spencer tilted his head, pausing as though sifting through memory. "There was one thing Dick told me."

Yuuto's heart skipped a beat—yet the words that came next weren't what he anticipated.

"He said you reminded him of a dog he had when he was a kid."

"A…dog?" Yuuto blinked. "But Dick grew up in an orphanage, didn't he?"

"Right. The dog was from there. Black as coal, no markings, no charm—didn't even like to be petted. But if you ignored it long enough, it'd stare at you from the shadows, like it was just waiting for you to notice it."

Yuuto frowned. "And this is supposed to mean something?"

"Dick said you were the same way."

Yuuto stared at him, lost for words, while Rob beside him choked back a laugh.

"Rob," Yuuto warned.

"Sorry," Rob managed, though his grin only widened. "But…I kind of see it. God, that's—"

He broke off, laughing again.

Yuuto glared at him, but Spencer wasn't finished.

"When you collapsed and they brought you here," Spencer went on, his voice softer now, "I'd never seen Dick so shaken. He was terrified for you. I don't think he even realized it himself, but that man would have burned this place down if it meant keeping you alive. You've both been through hell since then—your lives, your roles, everything's changed. But that feeling? That was real. No question about it."

Yuuto's chest tightened at the quiet certainty in Spencer's eyes. "Doctor," he asked, his voice lower now. "What kind of man was Dick to you?"

Spencer smiled faintly. "Is that the FBI talking?"

"No." Yuuto shook his head. "Just me."

"Let's see…" Spencer leaned back in his chair, gaze drifting toward the ceiling. "He had a sharp tongue and a cold demeanor, but beneath all that, Dick was a deeply compassionate man. The inmates in the infirmary—most of them cursed him out regularly—but every single one of them was grateful to him. When the pain got too much, when they couldn't bear it anymore, they always called for him. Like a child calling for their mother."

A faint smile flickered on Spencer's lips.

"I think they believed that if anyone could understand their suffering, it was Dick. He had that kind of presence. Strange man, really."

Yuuto silently agreed. Despite how cold Dick could seem, there was something about him that made people want to lean on him—something that made you want to surrender all your defenses and let him wrap you in that quiet, unspoken warmth.

Thinking of Dick hurt.

Yuuto forced himself to suppress the feeling, thanked Spencer, and left the infirmary.

Outside, Guthrie was waiting for them. As they stepped back into the corridor, Yuuto saw a familiar face approaching.

"Matthew?"

The young man looked up, surprised. His face was freckled and still boyish, almost childlike, with a slender, fragile frame. There was no mistaking him. It was Matthew Kane.

"Yuuto? Is it really you?" The moment recognition flashed in his eyes, Matthew's whole face lit up. He nearly skipped across the hallway and threw himself into Yuuto's arms.

Yuuto easily caught his slight frame, smiling. "Yeah, it's me. Good to see you, Matthew. When did you get back?"

Matthew was brutally assaulted by a Chicano inmate named Bernal and spent weeks recovering in an outside hospital. By the time he returned, Yuuto had already been released, without even a chance to say goodbye.

"About ten days ago, I guess," Matthew said. "When I came back, everyone was gone. I heard what happened, though—your name was cleared, and you got out. Congratulations."

"Thanks. And what about you? How's your health?"

"Good as new. I've even been helping out in the infirmary."

"Really? That's great. And the others? No one's been giving you trouble?" Yuuto asked, worry creeping into his voice. He couldn't help but imagine Matthew being targeted again.

"Nope." Matthew shook his head. "Actually…it's weird, but Alonso—the Chicano—he's been looking out for me. Thanks to him, nobody messes with me anymore."

Alonso…Yuuto remembered him. He was a high-ranking member of *Locos Hermanos* and one of Neto's most trusted men. For a second, Yuuto wondered why a Chicano gangster would bother protecting a White kid like Matthew, but then it clicked.

Neto.

Before Yuuto's release, he asked Neto to watch over Matthew—just enough to make sure the kid didn't get hurt again. Seeing Matthew safe and smiling now, Yuuto felt a wave of relief and deep gratitude for Neto's loyalty. The man had kept his word.

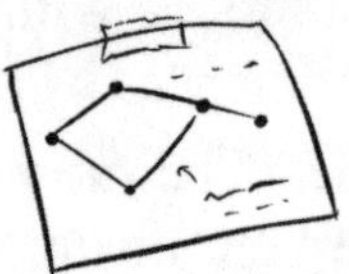

"Are you sure it's okay for me to stay here?" Yuuto asked.

"Okay? You've already checked out of your hotel," Rob said with a smirk. "There's no going back now."

"Well, yeah, but…I don't want to be a bother."

After returning to L.A., they had dinner in Chinatown before Yuuto officially checked out of his hotel and followed Rob back to his place. He initially refused Rob's invitation, but Rob was so persistent that Yuuto eventually gave in.

Sure, Rob's romantic intentions were obvious, but Yuuto knew he wasn't the type to push boundaries. That, at least, made him feel more at ease.

Seated on the couch across from him, Rob let out an exasperated laugh. "You worry too much. If I thought you were a bother, I wouldn't have invited you in the first place."

"Still…What if I'm in the way? You won't be able to bring anyone over."

"Don't start with that," Rob said, rolling his eyes. "You know I don't have a boyfriend. I've been single ever since I got dumped three months ago."

Yuuto arched an eyebrow. "Whoever dumped you clearly didn't appreciate what they had. Handsome, kind, and even capable of changing a baby's diaper like a pro—all while being a college professor. That's not exactly common."

"That might be the best compliment I've ever gotten." Rob tugged at his tie with a laugh before firing back. "What about you? No cute boyfriend waiting for you in New York?"

"If I had one, I wouldn't be sitting here drinking with you," Yuuto said dryly.

"Fair enough. Another glass?"

Before Yuuto could respond, Rob filled his empty glass with white wine.

"Speaking of phone calls," Rob said lightly. "That guy you were talking to earlier—Heiden, right? He's your direct supervisor?"

"Yeah," Yuuto said with a faint grimace. "He can be unbearable, but thanks to you, he was in an unusually good mood today. That Nathan interview you helped with must've really impressed him. He didn't even chew me out for coming back from Schelger Prison empty-handed."

Yuuto had already called Heiden the night before to ask for permission to include Rob in the investigation. Even after Yuuto explained that Rob was a criminologist who had worked with the FBI before, Heiden was still hesitant. However, when Yuuto mentioned that Rob had exclusive footage of Nathan's interview, Heiden's attitude completely changed. He not only granted permission but was likely still watching the footage now, scrutinizing every detail.

"Talking to the people involved directly is essential," Rob said, swirling the wine in his glass. "Sometimes the smallest words, the tiniest gestures, can be the key that cracks a case wide open."

Yuuto hadn't found anything useful in what Guthrie or Spencer had told them earlier. When he brought it up, Rob suggested that the real key might lie in the connection between Corvus and former warden Corning.

"From your perspective, what was their relationship like?" Rob asked.

"Relationship? One was a warden, the other a prisoner. They rarely crossed paths in front of me. But…there was one time," Yuuto murmured, memory surfacing. "Corning burst into the library where Corvus sat and tore into him with a fury I'd never seen."

"The warden went to him personally?" Rob leaned forward, clearly intrigued.

Yuuto nodded and described what he'd seen. As he recalled, Corning and Corvus had been arguing about Neto. It was around the time Neto—who had been kept in solitary confinement for a long stretch to prevent further clashes between the Black and Chicano inmates—was suddenly released back into the general population.

"Don't get full of yourself. Not everything goes the way you want. Just returning Rivera to the general population was already a major concession on our part."

Corning had snapped, his displeasure plain as day. Corvus—then still Nathan—simply replied in that calm, unshakable voice of his:

"Mr. Corning. I've explained many times that releasing Rivera, in the long run, will lead to positive outcomes for the prison as well.

When Yuuto finished recounting the exchange, Rob frowned. "That sounds like their roles were reversed. Like Corvus was the one in charge."

Back then, Yuuto hadn't thought much of it. Nathan had always been outspoken about prisoners' rights, so it didn't seem unusual that he was the one pushing Corning. If anything, it made sense that he would fight to get Neto out of solitary.

"If what you're saying is right," Rob mused, "then Corvus was the one who got Neto released. But why? What was his goal?"

Yuuto placed a hand on his forehead, closed his eyes, and

searched his memories. He was forgetting something important—something about what Corvus truly wanted.

Then, like a spark in the dark, Dick's voice echoed in his mind: *"Were you ordered to start the riot? Or is all this your own plan?"*

Yuuto's eyes snapped open.

"The riot," he said quietly. "Corvus wanted the riot to happen."

"The riot?" Rob asked. "Why?"

"I don't know why," Yuuto admitted, shaking his head. "But I'm sure of it. Dick said as much to him."

During the riot, Dick and Corvus finally unmasked each other. Yuuto remembered Dick, gun in hand, demanding to know if Corvus was the one who killed Choker, the Black gang leader who opposed the fighting. If Choker was gone, his ruthless second-in-command, BB, would take over, and with him in charge, the racial conflict between the Black and Chicano inmates would erupt.

Rob's expression darkened. "I see. So, Neto gets released, BB takes power, and tension between the Blacks and Chicanos skyrockets. That would definitely make a riot inevitable."

"Exactly. The question is—why did Corvus want that riot in the first place?"

"Because a riot would make it easier to escape? No…that doesn't add up," Rob muttered. "If Corvus really had Corning under his thumb, he wouldn't have needed such a messy distraction to walk out of that prison."

He leaned forward, his gaze sharp.

"Yuuto. The more information, the better. Tell me everything Corvus ever said to you—anything you remember."

"Yeah," Yuuto said with a small nod. "I wanted you to hear it all anyway."

He told Rob about his conversations with Corvus—how the man had sharply criticized the state of American prisons. Every year, inmate numbers climbed at an alarming pace. Yet what was rising wasn't crime, but incarceration. Driving that surge was the privatization of prisons, where corporations profited by deliberately inflating inmate populations.

"Corvus wasn't wrong," Rob admitted. "The prison-industrial complex has become a crucial part of this country's economy, for better or worse. You know, Yuuto, the reason I left Georgetown University was actually because of this exact issue. I clashed with another professor over prison privatization."

That confession caught Yuuto off guard. "What happened?"

"He was a renowned scholar and a vocal supporter of privatization, but behind the scenes, he was making large amounts of money from the Smith-Bucks Company."

"The same Smith-Bucks Company that runs Schelger Prison?"

"That's the one," Rob confirmed. "Technically, it wasn't illegal—the money was disguised as research funding and consulting fees. But he was still selling his work to line his own pockets. I'm not saying privatization should be completely dismissed… But I couldn't stomach his hypocrisy anymore. Corvus was right about one thing: this country's priorities are warped. Half the national budget gets funneled into dead-end sectors—law enforcement, the military, prisons. Before pouring billions into new facilities, shouldn't we be investing in schools and affordable housing? But profit runs everything. Laws are rewritten for it. Politicians and academics bow to it."

Yuuto silently topped off Rob's glass of wine. Rob looked momentarily embarrassed by his outburst and muttered an apology, and quickly added, "I'm not saying Corvus was right."

"I know," Yuuto murmured. "Corvus was just wearing the mask then—Nathan, the clever, respectable man people wanted to see. That wasn't him speaking."

He lingered over his wine, then whispered, "It was…a slip."

"A slip?" Rob asked, blinking. "What do you mean?"

"Dick told me once that Corvus had gotten so absorbed in playing Nathan that he started slipping, accidentally giving himself away. And Dick also said…" Yuuto hesitated, hearing the words again in his mind, "that Corvus was hiding in the shadows behind everything wrong with that prison."

"Hiding in the shadows?" Rob echoed, throwing his head back with a groan. "Why the hell did Dick always have to speak in riddles?"

"He was under contract with the CIA. He had an obligation to keep their secrets," Yuuto said softly. "That was probably the closest thing to a hint he could give me."

Dick had broken the rules for him—Yuuto was sure of it. He did it so Yuuto could stand on equal footing when negotiating with the FBI, allowing him to win his freedom with his own hands.

"Still drinking?" Rob asked, lifting the wine bottle.

Yuuto shook his head. "I'm done. I think I'm a little drunk."

"Then lie down if you want," Rob said. "Make yourself at home."

Yuuto accepted the offer. He pulled his legs up onto the sofa, resting an elbow on the backrest, and cradled his heavy head in his hand. A comforting haze washed over him, making it tempting just to drift off right there.

"Yuuto," Rob said after a moment, his tone shifting. "Mind if I ask you something…personal?"

Yuuto blinked lazily, signaling him to go ahead.

"Tell me what kind of relationship you and Dick really had."

CHAPTER 9

The question caught Yuuto off guard. He frowned slightly, not quite understanding what Rob was getting at.

"He was my cellmate. A CIA agent. He kept an eye on me because he thought I was working for the FBI," Yuuto replied. "Didn't I already explain that?"

"You did," Rob admitted. "But even so…you two were close. Closer than I'd expect from people who were supposed to be enemies."

"I didn't know Dick was CIA," Yuuto said.

"Sure," Rob allowed. "But he knew who you were, or thought he did. And Spencer swore he cared about you. And you…" Rob studied Yuuto for a moment. "Every time his name comes up, your face changes. Not pain, exactly. More like…sorrow. Like it aches, somewhere deep down."

Yuuto stared back at him, speechless. He hadn't realized it was that obvious. A restless feeling grew in his chest, and unease crept in, as if the ground beneath his feet had shifted. The warmth of the wine suddenly felt uncomfortable, heavy in his veins.

"Even enemies can become friends," Yuuto muttered at last.

"Just friends?" Rob asked softly.

The way Rob asked it—doubtful, probing—rattled Yuuto's nerves. Yuuto narrowed his eyes at him, showing his displeasure without trying to hide it. Rob didn't seem bothered in the slightest and kept going, "Maybe you and Dick had…a special kind of relationship."

Yuuto had already guessed where Rob was headed with this, so it didn't surprise him. Instead, what rose in his chest was anger—anger that demanded, *And what if we did?*

"What do you mean by 'special'? Don't beat around the bush. Just say it plainly."

Even Yuuto was surprised at how cold his voice sounded.

"Fine," Rob said evenly. "I've heard that in prison, even men who aren't gay sometimes have…compensatory sexual relationships. And other times, they're forced. Were you and Dick—"

"Cut the euphemisms. What you're really asking is if I slept with Dick, isn't it?"

Rob took a deep breath, staring intensely at Yuuto, who now returned his gaze with a sharp, defiant look. "I just want to understand how you feel about him—"

"You really are nothing but curiosity wrapped in skin, aren't you?"

Yuuto's tone grew rough, his irritation spilling through. But the anger wasn't aimed at Rob—it was directed entirely at himself. It disgusted him how easily Rob's words had struck a nerve and how quickly he'd lost control.

"What is this, Rob? Do you want to write a paper about it? Take me as your perfect case study for sexual behavior behind bars?"

"Yuuto, that's not what I—"

"If you really want to know, then fine. I'll tell you." Yuuto's voice cut through the air like glass. "While I was inside, I had sex with men. The first was BB, a Black gang member. He marked me, Rob. Told everyone he was gonna make me his bitch."

Fueled by the wine, Yuuto felt a bitter, self-destructive satisfaction twist in his gut, pushing the words out of his mouth like a blade against his own skin.

"They held me down in the shower. BB fucked me while the others pinned me against the wall. I passed out. They had to haul me to the infirmary, and I woke up to Spencer telling me he'd run tests to check if there was semen inside me. That's the kind of humiliation I lived through."

Rob flinched, but Yuuto wasn't done. He couldn't stop. His self-loathing had momentum now, and it drove him forward with a twisted kind of relief. "And after that, I slept with Dick too."

"Yuuto, that's enough—"

"No. You want to hear it? Then hear it." Yuuto's voice cracked, raw and vicious. "I begged him for it. I climbed onto his lap and told him to hold me like I was a woman. I wanted him, Rob. Even after I'd been raped, I still wanted him. I wanted him so badly it hurt. That's who I am."

His voice fell to a broken rasp. "That's the kind of man I am. Pathetic."

Yuuto pressed his right hand over his mouth, trying to hold back the storm inside him. But his hand trembled uncontrollably, as if convulsing.

Rob's eyes carried a look of sympathy, as if witnessing something painfully fragile. Yuuto instantly regretted his outburst, not because he was angry at Rob, but because he realized he still couldn't fully face the reality of what had happened to him in prison.

He wasn't sorry at all for having slept with Dick. He thought it was something they both needed at the time. Still, every time he remembered being with Dick, the memory of the rape came rushing in at the same time. Those two completely different experiences—consensual sex and sex by force—were deeply tangled inside him.

"I'm sorry, Rob…"

"It's okay. Don't worry about it. I was insensitive. You had every right to be angry."

Rob's kindness felt like a bittersweet stab to Yuuto's chest. He thought it might be easier if Rob looked at him with contempt instead.

"I'm not angry at you. I'm just…I can't forgive myself. I hate myself…"

As Yuuto bowed his head, Rob stood up and moved beside him, gently placing a hand on his shoulder and stroking his back to comfort him. Gradually, Yuuto's tension started to lessen under Rob's tender touch.

"You went through something terrible. If you want, I'm here to listen. Sometimes letting it out helps."

Yuuto leaned against Rob's shoulder, seeking comfort like a lifeline.

"Yuuto, you're the kind of person who tries to handle everything alone, even when it hurts, aren't you? People like that tend to bottle everything inside, and that's why they can't heal from their past. There are things you don't want to tell anyone, right?"

Rob's voice was steady, almost soothing, and Yuuto listened, motionless, unable to give even the smallest nod.

"Then try telling *yourself*. Tell yourself it was really hard, really painful. It's okay to feel sorry for yourself. You don't have to feel miserable. The only one who can comfort you from your past is the you that's here now."

Yuuto murmured softly, "I wonder if that's really true."

"It is." Rob pulled Yuuto closer, wrapping an arm around his shoulder.

"Rob…"

"Hm?"

"When you experience both something terrible and something good at the same time, what do you do? I can't separate the two. I want to hold on to the good, but the bad always comes back. Then the good also starts to hurt."

"Hm. Maybe in times like that, you just need to experience the good over and over again. Keep going back to it until the bad memories start to fade."

Yuuto offered a small, tearful smile and shook his head. "That's not something I can do. It's impossible."

"You don't have to answer if you don't want to, but your bad experience was being raped, and the good one was sleeping with Dick?"

Yuuto nodded quietly. He had already confessed so much—there was no point in hiding anything now.

"So, the guy you talked about at the club, the one who slept with a man even though he's not gay…that was you. Did you really like Dick that much?"

"Yeah. If not, I wouldn't have gone to bed with a man. All my life, I believed I was straight…until I met him."

"Did you join the FBI because you wanted to find him?"

"I still hope to see him again. I don't want to leave Dick in the past. This investigation isn't just about that, I know—but for me, pursuing Corvus and searching for Dick have always been bound together, two sides of the same coin."

"If you're not gay, why did you feel that way about Dick?" Rob's calm voice and warm presence felt comforting.

Yuuto felt like he could tell Rob everything. He spoke slowly about how he met Dick, how someone he initially thought was unpleasant gradually became someone he cared about. He described Dick's lonely childhood, the sympathy it awakened in him, and how every small kindness Dick offered had mattered more than words could say. In that warmth, Yuuto had found a sense of fulfillment he hadn't known he was missing.

"Sorry if this sounds harsh," Rob said once Yuuto had finished. "I believe it's true you felt a strong affection for Dick. But was it really romantic love? You'd suffered a huge psychological blow from being wrongfully imprisoned, and you were under immense pressure because of Corvus. You were thrown into a bizarre world where violence and rape were rampant. Even if you weren't aware of it, you must have been pushed to the edge."

"How does that relate to my feelings?"

"Have you heard of the suspension bridge theory? It's often called the suspension bridge effect. It's a theory that men and women who meet on a shaky suspension bridge are more likely to fall in love than those who meet on a normal bridge. Basically, your body is physically excited by the dangerous situation, but your brain mistakes the source of that excitement as the person in front of you. In the movie *Speed,* the heroine says couples who get together under extreme circumstances don't last—that's the same idea."

"So you're saying my feelings were just a misunderstanding?" Yuuto looked up at Rob, confused.

"When someone is mentally unstable and treated kindly, it's natural to want to depend on them. And in places without the opposite sex, pseudo-romantic feelings toward the same sex can easily develop. There's a chance that your feelings for Dick were temporary, a product of the environment and circumstances. You might have just ended up sleeping with him because of those pressures, and what you actually felt could have been friendship…" Rob trailed off, then continued his explanation. "If you were gay, I wouldn't say this. But if you're mistaken, I think it's better to realize it soon. Holding on to an illusion only prolongs the pain."

Listening to Rob's words, Yuuto found himself more and more confused about his own feelings.

Was it just a delusional romance born from a unique situation? If nothing had gone wrong, if they had simply lived normally as friends who got along well, would he really have let Dick captivate him so completely?

Yuuto shook his head and stopped thinking. No matter how much he questioned himself, no answers would come. There was nothing more mysterious in this world than his own heart.

"You're confusing me. At the club, you said love was simple, but now you say it might be an illusion…I don't get it."

"Exactly." Rob smiled cheerfully and patted Yuuto's knee. "I'm conflicted too. Maybe at the club I gave you a casual answer because it felt like someone else's problem. And now, maybe I'm trying to push you to give up on Dick by making my advice sound plausible. Either way, advice from a guy with an ulterior motive should be taken with a grain of salt."

Yuuto couldn't help but laugh. "That's ridiculous. Weren't you supposed to hide your personal motives?"

"I'm weak-willed."

Don't be so open about it, Yuuto thought with a wry smile.

Rob rested one arm on the back of the sofa and suddenly had a serious expression. "Somehow, I think I understand how Dick felt. Even though he saw you as an enemy, he couldn't just leave you alone."

"Are you saying I look unreliable?"

"Not exactly. But there's part of you that really triggers a man's protective instincts." Rob gave a slight smile and looked at Yuuto with an oddly seductive gaze. Usually, he only gave healthy smiles, so it was strange to see him show such charm in moments like this. "Back to what I was saying earlier. If you want to know if you're really gay, there's a quick way to find out."

Yuuto looked back at Rob cautiously. "What's that?"

"Try sleeping with a man other than Dick. If you find sex with other men enjoyable enough, then the chance you're gay is higher."

That was another opinion that made Yuuto wonder if Rob was serious or just joking. "Sorry, but I'm not ready to just try having sex with a man."

"Then how about just a kiss? If you can kiss a man deeply without feeling disgust or discomfort, that alone might be a good sign for understanding your sexuality."

"Even if it's just a kiss, who exactly am I supposed to try it with?"

"Me."

It wasn't surprising. Yuuto had been expecting that answer. "Rob, I told you not to try to persuade me."

"I don't think it's that serious. It's just a kiss, you know? Are you scared? Not confident you can keep your cool if you kiss me?"

Whatever he said, Rob always had a comeback. Yuuto didn't even want to get angry anymore. Even being annoyed felt like too much trouble.

"You really should try kissing me. If you hate it, you can push me away. But if you find yourself enchanted and feeling great, then there's a good chance you're gay."

"That's a pretty bold conclusion. You really want to kiss me that much?" Yuuto laughed and leaned his head against the back of the sofa.

Rob smiled and nodded. "Yeah, I do. Kissing me might change something. You might start to notice me more, and eventually, you might care about me more than Dick."

"You're not only an optimist, but also extremely confident. Sorry, but I'm not going to fall for you just because we kissed."

"You won't know unless you try. It's a chance to forget about Dick."

"If it were that easy to forget, I wouldn't be struggling."

"That's why you try. Come on, let's kiss," he whispered, drawing his face closer. Rob's hand gently stroked Yuuto's cheek. Somehow, it didn't feel unpleasant—was it because Yuuto was actually gay, or because he liked Rob?

He wasn't sure. But a spark of curiosity grew inside him. He wanted to find out how he'd feel kissing a man other than Dick. Rob's teasing words had planted the seed.

"You always talk your way into getting what you want, don't you?"

"No way. You're the first person I've ever had to use such a complicated method to get a kiss from."

They whispered so close their breaths nearly mingled. The sweetness of it wasn't unpleasant. Would kissing Rob really reveal anything to him?

"Since we're at it, you might as well enjoy it. You don't hate kissing, do you?" That low voice stirred something deep inside his chest. Being looked at with such gentle eyes made Yuuto feel strangely unsettled.

Rob didn't go straight for a full kiss. Instead, he gently caressed Yuuto's cheek and jaw with his lips. The tender touch and warm breath felt pleasantly ticklish.

Yuuto shut his eyes, bracing himself, until Rob's lips finally touched his. They kissed in light nibbles, gentle bites. To his surprise, no real disgust surfaced.

Rob's tongue slipped between Yuuto's slightly parted lips. Reflexively, Yuuto almost snapped his mouth shut tightly, but rejecting the kiss would ruin it. He forced himself to accept Rob's intrusion.

Their tongues intertwined, the strange slickness making Yuuto's body flush with sudden warmth. Instinctively, he pressed at Rob's chest, but Rob didn't yield. When Yuuto tried to turn his face away, Rob's hands closed around his forehead and cheeks, holding him fast, denying escape.

A muffled sound escaped his lips. Realizing he was actually feeling something from the kiss with Rob, Yuuto's body tensed in embarrassment.

Rob paused the kiss briefly and softly pressed his lips against Yuuto's earlobe. "Yuuto. It's not wrong to enjoy yourself a little. Just relax more…"

Yuuto shook his head, gasping for air. "Please stop now."

"No way. Just a little longer. I'm not satisfied yet."

The kiss resumed—this time deeper and more passionate than before. Rob's lips moved loudly, his tongue pressing so hard it almost hurt. His tongue dominated Yuuto's entire mouth, and the feeling was almost like being in the middle of sex—extremely sensual.

Though Yuuto tried to resist, his lips moved effortlessly, accepting Rob.

A small voice in the back of his mind warned, "Don't get carried away," but his body was overwhelmed by the skilled kiss. He wanted to savor this sweet pleasure more and more.

Could it be okay without Dick? Could he enjoy it with another man?

That's not it, Yuuto thought sharply, chiding himself the moment disappointment stirred. If he wanted, he could share pleasure with anyone. For satisfying desire, the partner didn't matter. But the one who fulfilled his heart was only Dick. The one his heart truly sought was Dick alone.

"Rob, that's enough. I—"

With his lips brushing Yuuto's neck, Rob whispered, "Want to keep going? You could try me in bed too. I promise, I won't disappoint—you might even be impressed with the size."

The crude joke from a university professor instantly killed the mood. Yuuto pushed Rob away and stood up.

"Yuuto?"

"Thanks, Rob. Because of you, I understand my feelings a lot better."

CHAPTER 10

Rob, sitting in the passenger seat, let out a big yawn. Yuuto glanced sideways at Rob's sleepy face while gripping the steering wheel. "You didn't have to force yourself to come along."

Rob frowned at Yuuto's cold words and tone. "Are you still mad about yesterday?"

"Oh? So you are aware you said something to make me angry?"

"That was just a harmless joke."

"That was the worst kind of joke," Yuuto replied coldly, keeping his eyes on the road. A guy bragging about his size to get someone into bed.

"But the kiss was good, wasn't it?" Rob smiled brightly.

Yuuto answered with a cold voice, "Yeah, it was. But I won't do it again. I like you, but it's not romantic."

"It's too early to decide that. If I could, I'd like to try having sex with you. Once I'm on equal footing with Dick, I want to ask you again who you prefer."

"Where do you even get that confidence? Damn it, you idiot!" Yuuto snapped—but not at Rob. Up ahead, a red pickup suddenly slammed its brakes. The road was clear, yet it crawled forward, slowing again without speeding back up. "What the hell is that guy doing?"

"Distracted driving. Look, over in the other lane, a cop car is pulling someone over."

"If you wanna watch that badly, pull over to the shoulder." Yuuto honked and stepped hard on the gas to pass the pickup. His

Camry surged forward, gliding onto the split from the Pasadena Freeway to Interstate 5. Southbound on the 5 would take them toward the west side of East L.A.

"Yuuto, there are a lot of cops around here. Watch your speed."

"If I say I'm chasing a suspect, they'll probably let me off."

"That's exactly why people hate the FBI."

"I hate them too, so I don't care."

The two of them had been like this since morning. At first glance, it might have seemed tense, but neither was serious. Rob was just going along with it to ease Yuuto's awkward mood. Deep down, Yuuto was grateful for Rob's way of matching his pace.

"So, what kind of guy is this Rivera? I mean, if he's the boss of a prison gang, he's gotta be pretty intimidating, right?"

"He's imposing, sure, but he doesn't posture or act high and mighty. Neto's a really good guy."

If anyone knew something about *Ara Roja*, the Chicano gang that dealt with Nathan, it would be Neto, who once led a large street gang himself. That's why Yuuto got Neto's address from Guthrie back at Schelger Prison.

He'd also asked the LAPD for information, but *Ara Roja* had nearly been wiped out in a gang war last year and had since fallen off police radar. As a result, even the authorities didn't know where the gang's former leaders were now.

"Even if he's a good guy, won't his attitude change when he finds out you're FBI?"

"That, I can't say for sure." Yuuto felt a twinge of unease. As loyal as Neto might be, his attitude could very well harden once he realized Yuuto was law enforcement. He had already prepared himself for the possibility of being turned away.

They exited I-5 and began driving through Boyle Heights, a predominantly Chicano neighborhood. As they moved east along

César Chávez Avenue, they saw many vibrant murals. These colorful graffiti pieces weren't just random scribbles; they often conveyed powerful messages and were an important part of Chicano culture.

"This area feels like Mexico. Look—every sign's in Spanish."

Given that roughly half of L.A.'s population was Hispanic, Spanish wasn't unusual here. You could even take your driver's test in Spanish, and if you called customer service, the first automated prompt was always to choose between English and Spanish. But most White residents didn't go out of their way to visit East L.A. or South Central unless they had a reason—both areas had a reputation for being unsafe. For someone like Rob, this was a rare sight.

When they got to their destination, they parked on the street and began walking.

"'This must be the apartment, huh?" Rob said as he looked up at the shabby building.

Yuuto, however, noticed a bakery right next door and went inside. The Chicano woman behind the counter looked at Yuuto's note and confirmed that, yes, it was definitely the building next door.

Thanking her, Yuuto pushed open the glass door of the bakery—when he suddenly noticed a tall man walking behind Rob. The man wore a black baseball cap, jeans, and an olive-green military jacket, heading toward the main street with his back turned to Yuuto.

Yuuto's gaze was immediately fixed on the man's broad back.

He looks like Dick.

"Yuuto, is this the right place?" Rob's voice snapped Yuuto out of his thoughts, and he nodded.

"Yeah. This is the place, no doubt about it."

As they climbed the stairs to the apartment's porch, Yuuto

reassured himself that it was only his imagination. The man from earlier had the same vibe, but his hair was a dark brown. Besides, there was no way Dick would be here, of all places.

Neto's apartment was right at the top of the stairs. When Yuuto knocked, the door cracked open slightly, revealing a young Chicano man with a mustache peeking out. He asked in Spanish what they wanted. Yuuto responded in Spanish, saying he wanted to see Rivera.

"Do you have an appointment?" The young man's piercing gaze held open suspicion.

Yuuto could sense the tension behind his guarded tone. "No, I don't. But I know him. Just tell him Yuuto's here."

"No deal. Nobody gets to see Rivera without an appointment. Get lost."

Just as the man was about to shut the door, another voice called from inside, "Pepe. Who is it?"

Yuuto froze. He knew that voice.

"Neto, it's me! Yuuto!"

"Yuuto?" Through the narrow gap between the door and the frame, Yuuto finally saw Neto's surprised face. The young man muttered something to him before removing the door chain. The door swung open wide, and at last Yuuto stood face-to-face with Neto.

But then, Neto said something completely unexpected. "Dick was here. He just left."

"What?" Yuuto's eyes widened.

Seeing his reaction, Neto looked puzzled, as if he'd just realized he had misunderstood something. "Wait, you weren't here looking for him?"

Before Yuuto could even think, his body was already moving.

"Yuuto?" Rob shouted after him, but Yuuto didn't stop. He

sprinted down the stairs and out into the street.

It *was* Dick. He hadn't imagined it. Those shoulders. That back. No mistaking it.

Yuuto sprinted straight down the main street, frantically glancing left and right. Among the crowd on the sidewalk, there was no sign of anyone who looked like Dick.

Taking a chance, Yuuto turned right and ran. His eyes darted everywhere, searching desperately, praying he wouldn't lose him. He ran far down the street, but Dick was nowhere in sight.

Just as he was about to give up and turn back in defeat, he spotted it—a black baseball cap bobbing in the crowd ahead. Yuuto pushed past pedestrians, ignoring the angry shouts that followed him. The man was getting closer and closer. Military jacket. Same as before.

"Dick!"

Please, stay still. Don't go anywhere. He called out the name like a prayer.

The man turned around. His cap was pulled low, and black sunglasses obscured most of his face, but Yuuto didn't need to see more. There was no doubt.

It was Dick.

Dick Burnford.

"Dick, wait!" Yuuto barely managed to say before the man suddenly quickened his pace, moving away from him, escaping.

"Damn it!" Yuuto bolted after him, but by the time he reached the spot, Dick was gone. Maybe he had slipped into a side street. Yuuto checked every alley he passed, but no luck. No matter how far he ran, Dick was nowhere to be found.

Breath ragged, Yuuto stopped, stunned and still as the crowd moved past him. People looked at him warily and suspiciously before they went on.

He'd been so close. He'd seen Dick with his own eyes, and yet… he'd lost him. But what hurt the most wasn't losing sight of him. It was that Dick had run. Dick had seen him—and still ran.

Yuuto's legs felt heavy enough to buckle, but he forced himself to stand and gradually made his way back the way he had come. Each step felt like it was sinking into the pavement.

When he finally got to the apartment and knocked on the door, the young man from earlier peeked out and let him in.

Inside, Rob sat in a chair, but his face was unusually tense. Then Yuuto saw why—another man stood beside him, aiming a gun directly at Rob's head.

Yuuto snapped in sharp Spanish, "Put that damn thing down!"

The man ignored Yuuto's words and didn't move at all. Neto sat quietly on the other side of the table, watching.

"Neto, call him off. He's my friend. He's not suspicious."

"Can you prove that?"

"I just told you he's my friend. Isn't my word good enough?"

"I trust you," Neto said evenly. "But I don't know this man."

Yuuto let out a weary sigh at Neto's caution and turned to Rob. "Rob. Do you have anything on you that can prove your identity?"

"Yeah. My driver's license and my faculty ID are in my breast pocket."

Rob began to reach for them, but Neto's sharp voice cut through the room. "Don't move. Pepe. You do it."

The man with the gun, Pepe, reached into Rob's pocket and pulled out a bifold card case. He handed it to Neto, who examined the IDs. Satisfied that Rob was who Yuuto said he was, Neto ordered his men to leave the room.

Standing up, Neto returned the card case to Rob and then moved toward Yuuto. "Sorry about that, Yuuto. I didn't mean to treat your friend so rudely."

"It's fine. I should be the one apologizing for dropping in unannounced," Yuuto said with a forced, tired smile as he looked up at Neto.

In Neto's eyes, there was a quiet, almost pitying sympathy. "You didn't manage to see him, huh?"

"Do you know how to contact Dick?"

"No. He didn't say a word about that. Don't look like that. You should be happy. It's been a long time since you've seen him, right?" Neto's voice was gentle, the kind that seemed to seep into Yuuto's chest and ease the ache there.

It was overwhelming.

Yuuto clenched his teeth and fought back the flood of emotion. As if to say "don't hold it in," Neto wrapped an arm around Yuuto's head and drew him close against his chest. "You'll see him again someday. If it's Dick, you will."

"Neto…" Yuuto took several deep breaths, forcing himself to calm down. To show he truly was okay now, Yuuto lifted his head and gave Neto's chest a gentle pat. "Congratulations on getting out. I'm glad to see you looking well."

"Yeah. I'm glad to see you again, too."

"Let me introduce you properly. This is Rob Connors. He's a university professor."

"A professor, huh?" Although there was still a hint of wariness in his attitude toward Rob, Neto respected Yuuto enough to extend his hand. "I'm Ernesto Rivera. Call me Neto."

"Thanks. I was honestly bracing myself, thinking today might be my last." Rob smiled as he shook it. "After scaring me like that, the least you could do is pour me a cup of coffee, don't you think?"

At Rob's shamelessness, Neto furrowed his brow but said nothing; he simply brewed them some café de olla. It's a coffee traditionally enjoyed in Mexico, simmered with dark sugar and cinnamon. Its sweet aroma eased some of the heaviness in the air.

"How's Tonia doing?"

Tonia was Neto's younger transgender sister who had been at Schelger Prison but was moved to a federal facility after the riot. She remained strikingly beautiful and seductive enough to rival any woman, and she was also kind-hearted, looking after everyone. That's why she was affectionately called "Big Sister Tonia."

"I went to visit her the other day. She said the commissary at the federal prison is as well-stocked as a Kmart. She's almost out, too. When she gets released, she's going to live with me."

"That's good. I'm sure Tonia's been waiting for that day."

"But how did you even find my address?"

As if recalling something, Neto asked the question, and Yuuto hesitated before answering.

"Well…" He knew he'd have to say it sooner or later. Steeling himself, he pulled out his badge and showed it to Neto. "I'm with the FBI now."

Neto furrowed his brow, glancing at the ID card with Yuuto's photo. His stern look caused Yuuto's chest to tighten. "I just got out of prison, and you're here to arrest me already?"

"No, that's not—" Yuuto quickly tried to deny it, but then saw Neto's eyes laughing. He was teasing him. "You still think of me as a friend?"

"Of course. You've got yourself an honorable job."

Relieved that Neto's attitude remained unchanged, Yuuto was caught off guard when Rob suddenly interrupted.

"Doesn't it bother you?" Rob asked. "I mean, you were the boss of a prison gang, weren't you? I've also heard you used to run a pretty big street gang."

Neto cast a cool glance at Rob, who had interrupted. "In prison, you need an organization to protect yourself. And every organization needs someone to keep it together. Back in Schelger

Prison, I just happened to be the one who was suited for it. That's all in the past now."

"But even now, you're still...well, what should I call it..." Rob struggled for a second to find the right words. "Active, right?"

Despite Rob's blunt question, Neto stayed calm and nodded. "More or less. I'm still part of the organization, sure. But before I went to prison, I stepped down from the top position myself. These days, I'm more like an advisor to the younger guys."

"You might think you've retired, but I bet your people still see you as their boss." Rob eyed him suspiciously. "I mean, what kind of 'advisor' walks around with two bodyguards?"

Neto, looking troubled, turned his gaze toward Yuuto. "Does this professor have it out for me or something?"

"Rob doesn't mean anything by it. He's just insatiably curious." Yuuto hesitated briefly before shifting the topic. "Neto, can I ask you something? Why was Dick here?"

He needed to know, but Neto's expression hardened.

"He asked you not to tell anyone, didn't he?"

"Yeah. He made me promise I wouldn't tell a soul," Neto said, shaking his head. "I owe him a lot, Yuuto. So even if it's you, I can't say a word. Sorry."

Yuuto understood Neto's sense of loyalty well. No matter how much he begged, Neto wouldn't break his promise once he made up his mind. "I get it. I won't ask again, but just one thing—was Dick doing okay?"

There was a strange pause. "Yeah. He was okay."

Yuuto looked into Neto's dark eyes, suspicion gnawing at him. "Really? He didn't seem...different in any way?"

Neto didn't answer, and that only made Yuuto more anxious.

"Don't tell me he was hurt or something?"

"No. It's not that. It's just—well, how do I put it..." For once,

Neto, who was usually never at a loss for words, seemed to struggle to express himself. "His way of talking and acting was the same as before, but to me, he felt like a completely different person."

"A different person? You mean because he dyed his hair and disguised himself?"

"His appearance has changed a bit, sure, but that's not it. It's his presence. He's always had this unique aura, like he was shutting everyone else out, even back when we were in prison," Neto explained with a faraway look. "But when I saw him today, it felt even stronger. Maybe it's because of life on the run. If you're constantly being hunted, it'll put you on edge."

Yuuto didn't think that was it. It wasn't because Dick was being hunted; Dick was the hunter. If you spent every day focused solely on the man you wanted to kill, it was only natural that you'd radiate a harsh, almost violent air.

For Dick, chasing Corvus wasn't just a job or obligation. He simply wanted to kill the man who murdered his friends and his lover. If that was all that motivated him now, Yuuto's chest tightened at that thought.

Was hatred and the desire for revenge really the only things keeping him going? Would there ever be peace for him until he achieved that goal?

"Has Dick been in L.A. ever since he broke out of prison?"

Perhaps considering this question harmless enough, Neto shook his head. "No. It seems like he's been away from L.A. most of the time. He's only here temporarily. He said that once he's done with his business, he's leaving right away."

That made sense. With the police watching the city closely, it would be risky for Dick to move around L.A. unnecessarily. For him to return now, there had to be something important, something tied to Corvus.

"This coffee's great." Rob, completely unfazed, held out his cup with a relaxed smile. "Mind if I get a refill?"

"You've got some nerve, professor," Neto muttered with a scowl, but he still stood up to pour more coffee.

As Neto headed to the kitchen, Yuuto remembered why he was really here. "Neto, do you know a gang called *Ara Roja*?"

"*Ara Roja*? Yeah, those guys from South Central. I heard they used to make a killing dealing drugs, but didn't they get wiped out in a gang war?"

"That's what I've heard. What I want to know is about when they were at their peak—back when they were pushing a lot of cocaine. I'm looking for the man who was supplying them. Any idea who that might be?"

Neto handed Rob a fresh cup of coffee, then sat down and stroked his chin thoughtfully. "I don't know them directly, so I probably can't help you… But Chente might know something."

"Chente? Who's that?"

"You know him also. Alonso. Vicente Alonso."

"Oh, from *Locos Hermanos*…" Yuuto mused. "Come to think of it, I met Matthew back in Schelger Prison. He said Alonso was looking out for him. You asked him to, didn't you? Thanks."

"It was nothing."

"So, what's Alonso's connection to *Ara Roja*?"

"Chente himself isn't involved, but his cousin used to be part of *Ara Roja*. He's gone straight now and lives in San Diego, if I remember correctly. If you're okay with that, I can ask Chente to get in touch and find out some information."

"Please. Anything at all would help—whoever was involved in the cocaine trade, names, organizations, whatever you can find."

"Got it," Neto said. "Where should I contact you?"

Yuuto gave him his cell phone number, as well as Rob's home address and phone number.

"I'm staying at Rob's place for now," Yuuto explained.

Rob smiled warmly at Neto. "How about you come over for dinner sometime? I'd really love to hear about your experiences. I'm fascinated. I'll draw you a map, so you can't say no, alright?"

Without waiting for an answer, Rob cheerfully began sketching on a piece of paper, humming to himself.

"Your friend is a strange one."

"I think so too."

Yuuto and Rob left Neto's apartment and returned to their car. As Yuuto closed the passenger-side door, his phone rang from inside his suit jacket. He checked the display, but what he saw was an odd number that started with 000.

Suspicious, he brought the phone to his ear. "Hello?"

A voice answered. "Yuuto?"

A surge of tension raced through his whole body. His heartbeat sped up.

Could it really be?

"It's you, isn't it, Yuuto? Say something." The voice spoke like that of an old friend.

In Yuuto's mind, a familiar face appeared instantly.

"Nathan. Or should I say Corvus?" Yuuto finally answered. "It's been a while."

Rob's expression in the driver's seat changed at Yuuto's words.

"I don't like that name. Call me Nathan, like you used to."

"I can't. You're not the real Nathan. How did you get this number?"

"Does that really matter? More importantly, congratulations on getting out. I'm truly glad your innocence was proven. In a way, I feel vindicated." His gentle tone and soft voice were the same as ever, but now that Yuuto knew the truth, they struck him as grotesque.

"I was always innocent. But you weren't. You called it a false accusation, but you killed Nathan's mother, didn't you?"

"I've already forgotten. You can't expect me to remember someone so meaningless forever."

He killed someone, and now he says he's forgotten? Whether it was a joke or not, rage surged in Yuuto's chest. "Then what about the real Nathan? What was he to you?"

On the other end of the line, Corvus let out a low laugh. "The same. I never felt anything special for him. He was just convenient, so I used him. But his death wasn't pointless. He was useful to me in the end."

So Nathan was dead after all. Yuuto had suspected it, but hearing the truth directly from Corvus sent a fresh wave of fury through him.

"Yuuto. Don't you want to know where Nathan is now?"

Yuuto held the phone so tightly it creaked, trying to keep his voice steady. "I do. Where did you hide his body?"

"Go to San Gabriel Cemetery in Monterey Park. You'll find his grave there. I gave him a proper burial," Corvus spoke happily. "I even left you a small gift as a congratulations for getting out. I hope you like it."

The call ended suddenly. Yuuto clicked his tongue and lowered the phone from his ear.

Rob, watching him closely, immediately asked, "What did Corvus say? Why did he call you?"

"Rob, could this number be from Skype?" Yuuto showed Rob the incoming number.

"Yeah." Rob nodded. "That's a dummy number from Skype. He must've used SkypeOut to call."

Skype was an internet-based IP phone service that allowed users to make free calls to each other worldwide. Using the SkypeOut feature, you could also call regular landlines and cell phones.

"Smart. Skype calls are almost impossible to trace. You can't identify the user from a number like this."

"Couldn't we just ask Skype headquarters for the caller information?"

"The call charges are paid by credit card. If he used a fake card, it's hopeless."

Which meant they couldn't track Corvus down from the phone call. Grinding his teeth in frustration, Yuuto fastened his seatbelt.

"Corvus said Nathan's grave is at San Gabriel Cemetery in Monterey Park. He also said he left something there for me."

"All right, let's go." Rob dropped the handbrake and pressed down on the accelerator.

CHAPTER 11

"And what's Nathan Clark's body doing all the way out here?"

"I don't know," Yuuto answered. "But the man suspected of killing Nathan said so. It's highly reliable information, so we have to confirm it no matter what."

Even after hearing Yuuto's explanation, Paco's face stayed grim. In front of their gaze, LAPD officers with jackets bearing the LAPD logo held shovels, digging up the dirt.

After Yuuto's call, Paco convinced his boss to send a team of about a dozen officers to the scene right away.

"Sorry for bothering you when you're busy, Paco," Yuuto apologized.

Finally, Paco's expression softened. "Why are you apologizing? If the real Nathan Clarke is there, this is serious. The only thing that bothers me is that FBI agents are here. They just boss people around and don't seem genuinely interested in helping."

True to Paco's words, the FBI agents stood back and let the LAPD officers work. Still, they couldn't resist offering their opinions, which quickly grated on Paco.

When Yuuto and the others reached San Gabriel Cemetery, they moved across the large grounds and finally found a tombstone engraved with Nathan's name. The birth year matched, and the death year was two years ago. Additionally, the stone bore a sarcastic epitaph.

He was reborn and continues to live.

Convinced it was the correct grave, Yuuto requested backup

from the LAPD and also contacted Heiden in D.C.. Following Heiden's orders, FBI agents from the Los Angeles office arrived as well.

"I had the cemetery managers contact the owner of the plot, but they said they had no recollection of purchasing it," Paco said.

"Maybe someone used the name without permission," Rob replied to Paco's words. "Then the death certificate and burial permit might be forged, too."

Mike, who came along with them, shook his head in confusion next to Paco. "Why go through all that trouble? If the body was in the way, why not just dump it in the ocean or the mountains?"

"Who knows? Maybe it was the culprit's warped sense of mercy."

"This makes no sense at all… Oh, I see the vault."

Beneath the dirt, a vault—a container made to hold a coffin and keep out dirt and water—was uncovered. The vault's lid was lifted, revealing the coffin inside. The officers securely tied ropes around the coffin and carefully lifted it out with a crane truck.

When the coffin was placed on the grass, everyone present gathered around.

"Ugh, I won't be eating any meat today," Mike muttered, making the sign of the cross with his fingers.

Yuuto felt a heavy weight in his chest, knowing he was about to see a gruesome corpse. Normally, embalming is done before a funeral, but in Nathan's case, it's highly likely he was buried as-is. After two years, the body would have already begun to turn to bones.

"Paco, open it."

The officers overseeing the work placed their hands on the lid of the coffin. When Paco gave the signal, the lid was lifted, exposing the inside of the coffin.

"Whoa!"

"Ah!"

The officers holding the lid stumbled backward, falling onto their backs as if their knees had given out. They weren't the only ones shocked. Yuuto almost screamed too.

Most of the men present were no strangers to dead bodies. Had the corpse been decomposed or reduced to bones, they wouldn't have been shocked. But what lay inside was nothing like they expected. The man in the coffin was far too strange. Likely, everyone there had the same thought:

This wasn't a corpse.

"Hey, wait—could this guy still be alive?" Mike leaned in to look into the coffin with a worried expression. He said aloud what everyone else had been thinking.

Because the real Nathan lay there, eyes wide open. His cheeks had a faint flush, and he looked like he could sit up at any moment. A corpse inside the coffin, staring up at the sky with what looked like a faint smile.

It was nightmarish.

"Check if he's breathing."

"He's dead. There's no doubt about it. Look, there's a bullet wound on his forehead." Rob said this.

Mike twisted his lips awkwardly and muttered, "You know… cases like this do happen sometimes. People get buried in a state close to death and later come back to life. His eyes look clear—I've never seen a corpse like this."

"Excuse me." Rob pushed Mike aside, wrapped his handkerchief around his hand, and gently lifted Nathan's eyelids. "This is a glass eye…an elaborate embalming trick, but in terrible taste. If the goal were only to keep the lids from sinking, an ordinary eye cap would have done. Instead, it makes him look as if even in death he wasn't allowed any peace."

Rob spoke with a tone full of indignation as he gently covered Nathan's face with his handkerchief. Later, Nathan's body, wrapped in a plastic sheet, was carried to the transport vehicle under FBI orders.

"Hey, Doc, is it really possible to preserve a corpse that cleanly?" Mike asked.

"Yeah," Rob answered. "Depending on the preservation method, even standard embalming can keep a body intact for several years. With proper treatment, it could have remained that way for thirty to fifty years."

"That's the culprit's twisted sense of mercy again," Mike grumbled.

"No, this is desecration," Rob spat back coldly. "It looks like they're playing with a corpse. The fact that they deliberately didn't fix the most obvious wound on the forehead is proof of that."

In an instant, the cemetery transformed into a crime scene. Yellow tape blocked off all access, and the atmosphere became chaotic.

Yuuto led Rob to a spot a bit farther away. "Did you see Nathan's clothes? They were the same ones he wore when you interviewed him."

"Yeah. I noticed too. Maybe Nathan was killed right after he met me."

Yuuto's phone rang. The caller ID displayed that familiar number starting with zero again.

"Corvus?"

"Probably," Yuuto replied and picked up the phone.

"Hey, Yuuto. Have you met the real Nathan yet?" Corvus's cheerful voice sounded as if he were asking whether Yuuto was having a good time at a party.

"Tell me why you buried Nathan in the cemetery."

"They say if you want to hide leaves, hide them in the forest. A cemetery isn't a strange place to find a body."

"Then why tell me now?"

"Because I no longer have to be Nathan," Corvus explained matter-of-factly. "Also, I wanted to let you take credit. Investigators who don't make progress have a hard time."

Yuuto wondered how Corvus knew he had joined the FBI. When Yuuto remained silent, Corvus kept talking.

"Do you remember I said I had a gift for you? Somewhere there's a grave with a bouquet of red roses. Find it. Oh, but listen carefully first." A faint click followed, as if a button had just been pressed. "Hear that? That was the detonator. The bomb hidden in the bouquet will go off in one minute."

Yuuto was stunned by the words he could hardly believe. Corvus let out a low laugh. "Is there anyone nearby? Fifty seconds left."

Yuuto reacted instantly. Still clutching his phone, he shouted to Paco, who was speaking with officers a short distance away. "Paco! There's a bomb in this cemetery—in a bouquet of red roses! Evacuate everyone, *now*!"

"What?!"

"There's no time! It's about to go off!"

Hearing Yuuto's words, the officers froze with shocked expressions.

"Hey, is there a bouquet of red roses anywhere?" Paco scanned the area with his eyes, and others followed suit. There were several graves with flowers, but no bouquet of red roses nearby.

Time was running out. Yuuto clutched his phone tightly and began jogging around to search.

"Yuuto, look over there," Rob said, pointing.

Yuuto glanced over and saw Mike approaching, still fumbling

with his zipper—he'd clearly just relieved himself. Yuuto's throat tightened. Behind him, a splash of red flowers came into view. From this distance, he couldn't tell if they were roses, but there was no time to hesitate.

"Mike! Bomb!" Yuuto shouted at the oblivious Mike, who was approaching them with a casual expression.

"Huh? What did you say?"

"Just get down! There's a bomb in the red roses behind you! Get down now!!"

Mike glanced back, spotted the red roses, and shouted, "Whoa!" before hurling himself headfirst onto the grass.

A deafening explosion split the air. Yuuto flinched, turning his face away as he threw his arms over his head. Shards of tombstone and clumps of dirt rained down around them.

The smell of gunpowder lingered in the air as Yuuto pressed his hands to his ears and rushed to Mike, who was still lying on the ground.

"Mike, are you okay?"

"Damn it, my ears are ringing."

Paco hurried over and helped Yuuto lift Mike. Luckily, Mike had no serious injuries and was okay. If he had stayed standing, the blast wind probably would have knocked him over.

"Contact headquarters!"

"Call the bomb disposal team immediately!"

After the body was discovered, a bombing incident erupted, throwing the cemetery into chaos. Yuuto looked at the phone still clenched in his hand. The call was still connected.

"Corvus?" Yuuto said.

A whisper came back. "Yeah. Nice sound, wasn't it? But that was only an appetizer. I've prepared something better—something big. When it goes off, a lot of people will die."

A chill ran down Yuuto's spine. "Stop this foolishness right now!"

"I can't stop it anymore," Corvus said. "The next bomb is on a timer—set to go off exactly at three o'clock."

"Where—"

"*'Alpha'* was meant to be the finale, but for you, I'll leave a special mark in L.A. too," Corvus broke in with an eerie force, his words coiling like riddles in the dark. "I like you, Yuuto. I love that foolishness of yours, how you keep clawing your way toward the light, refusing to be swallowed by the darkness, even when the world treats you unfairly. I miss the time we spent together more than I can say. I'm glad I didn't kill you back then. I truly mean that. I'm always thinking of you. So I want you to think of no one but me."

"Cut the nonsense!" Yuuto shouted, his voice trembling. "Where's the bomb?"

"It's okay. There's still over an hour left. If you work hard, you can stop it."

"Don't joke with me…" His fists trembled as anger grew.

"Think of it as a game. Remember the poker we used to play in prison? It was fun regardless of who won, right? If you'd like to join the game between me and Dick, you're more than welcome."

Yuuto suppressed his raging emotions and took deep breaths. "Where is it planted? If this is a game, deal me a card."

Hearing this, Corvus chuckled softly. "You're right. Games aren't fun unless they're fair. Here's a hint: It's somewhere downtown."

"That's not enough. The odds are too heavily stacked against me."

"Then here's one more hint. The bomb is hidden in a place tied to your Japanese heritage."

"What?"

"You once said you felt your identity as a Japanese person was lacking. That's a sad thing. Even if you don't feel it, the history of your people still runs in your blood. So go to that place—and remember the suffering the Japanese community once endured. Good luck."

"Wait—" The call suddenly ended again. Furious, Yuuto punched his own leg with his fist. "Damn it!"

"Yuuto, what's wrong?" Paco grabbed Yuuto's arm, trying to calm him down. "Who were you talking to? Is it connected to the explosion earlier?"

Yuuto bit his lip and looked at Paco. "Paco. There is another bomb planted somewhere downtown. It's bigger than the last one. It's set to explode exactly at three o'clock."

"What?" Stunned, Paco stood silently as Yuuto rushed to explain.

"We need to head downtown right away. If we don't find it quickly, things will get bad…"

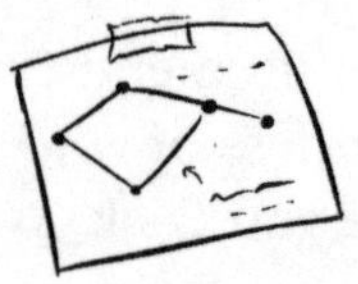

"A place fitting for someone of Japanese heritage?" Rob muttered, gripping the Camry's steering wheel, his brow furrowed. "Where could it be—Little Tokyo? A Japanese company building? The New Otani Hotel? The Japanese Consulate? Hmm…"

Ahead of them, a police car sped past with its siren blaring. Yuuto and the others followed closely, heading downtown with the police.

Sitting in the passenger seat, Yuuto nervously bit his nails. His mind was filled with Corvus's words. "He said the history of my people flows through my blood, to remember the painful past of the Japanese community. Maybe it's somewhere with historical significance."

"A place of historical significance..." Rob repeated thoughtfully. "When it comes to the painful past of Japanese Americans, the first thing that comes to mind is the World War II internment camps."

After Japan's attack on Pearl Harbor, the United States entered World War II. In 1942, Japanese Americans were forcibly detained in internment camps across roughly ten locations nationwide, with numbers reaching as high as 120,000. Those imprisoned lost the businesses and properties they had built. The policy affected not only immigrants from Japan but also second- and third-generation Japanese Americans who were U.S. citizens.

"But there's no internment camp ruins downtown."

"Then maybe a museum that teaches about that history?"

Yuuto suddenly realized and spun toward Rob. "That's it. It has to be there!"

"Where?"

"The Japanese American National Museum in Little Tokyo has many exhibits on Japanese American culture and history. It best fits Corvus's words."

"Makes sense," Rob agreed. "Yuuto, call Paco and tell him to head directly to the Japanese American National Museum. Also, have them secure the building and the surrounding area."

"But what if I'm wrong?"

"If you can't think of any other place, you have to bet on it. Evacuating the entire downtown area is impossible."

Prompted by Rob's strong words, Yuuto called Paco. After hearing the situation, Paco quickly agreed to send officers to the scene. Since the museum was just a short distance from the LAPD station, anyone inside could be evacuated swiftly.

The patrol car exited the freeway and turned south onto Alameda Street. Rob followed closely behind without letting any space come between them. Soon the Japanese American National Museum came into view.

When they arrived, several patrol cars were already gathered near the museum, and traffic was restricted. The entire area was tense. Yuuto and the others got out of the car, met with Paco, and entered the museum.

Haig, Paco's superior, stood in the lobby, giving stern orders to his subordinates. "Don't touch any suspicious objects! Send more officers to the second floor!"

Yuuto hardly greeted anyone and started searching the museum. Although he told others to stay outside for safety, Rob forced his way in to help with the investigation.

They searched everywhere—the exhibit halls, the gift shop, the administration offices—but found nothing suspicious. Yuuto moved from the main building to the new wing, running between the officers and frequently checking his watch to monitor the remaining time.

Only fifteen minutes were left. The growing sense of urgency intensified with each passing second.

Paco ran over, sweat gleaming on his forehead, and told him with frustration, "Yuuto, five minutes left to evacuate. Ten minutes before the explosion, everyone except the bomb squad has to be out."

It couldn't be helped. If they stayed, too many officers would get caught in the blast. Just as Yuuto was about to nod, a strained shout rang out from downstairs.

"I-I found it! I found it!"

Turning around, Yuuto saw a young officer with his head under a large display case. Paco and Yuuto raced down the stairs and looked underneath the exhibit at the same time.

"A plastic bomb?" Paco muttered, a chill running through him.

The entire underside of the display was covered with white packages tightly taped down with duct tape, and wires extended from them. Nearby, a detonator and a timer were attached. With this much explosive, the whole building could have blown apart.

Paco immediately reported the discovery of the bomb over the radio. The bomb disposal team, suited up in blast-resistant gear, arrived and started working. Everyone else was told to evacuate outdoors, so Yuuto and the others moved across the street to watch the new wing from outside.

Yuuto glanced at his watch—only four minutes left, and there was still no word on whether the device had been disarmed.

"Hey, is this really going to be okay?" Mike's voice was shaky.

Rob answered quietly, "If it's a normal plastic bomb, they just have to pull the fuse from the main body. But maybe there's some special rigging."

"Two minutes remaining. It's almost too late. Maybe they should evacuate the bomb squad too—"

Just as Yuuto spoke to Paco, a radio message crackled through. It was from the bomb squad—good news. The detonator had been successfully disabled.

"We did it! We did it!" Mike pumped his fist in the air. The officers nearby erupted in cheers. People hugged and shook hands, sharing their relief and joy.

Yuuto exhaled a sigh of relief and dropped to his knees. The idea that his very existence had provoked Corvus and caused this chaos weighed heavily on him, and he hadn't felt at ease until now.

Thank goodness.

They stopped the explosion without a single casualty. As Yuuto's mind settled, a deep, uncontrollable rage toward Corvus welled up inside him. Was Corvus's real aim simply to mock him and the police? If he had truly wanted the bombing to succeed, he wouldn't have left clues pointing to the bomb's location.

But Yuuto was sure that Corvus didn't mind if it exploded anyway. He appeared to be enjoying the thrill of the contest, whether Yuuto would win or Corvus himself.

Dick had said Corvus had blown up one of his own comrades half-jokingly, but now Yuuto understood that statement with chilling clarity. Corvus was a madman who treated human life like a toy.

Whenever Yuuto thought about Corvus, Nathan's gentle face appeared in his mind, and deep down, he tended to see them as different people. But after this ordeal, the two faces that had been separated finally came together clearly.

Yuuto shook his head so violently it looked as if it might come off. Just then, Haig appeared. Yuuto rose to thank him, but Haig spoke first. "Good work, Yuuto. Come by the station later—we need to discuss why the perpetrator chose to call you with the threat."

"There's no need for that," Agent Jefferson cut in from behind. "This is the same suspect behind a series of bombings across the United States. The FBI is handling the investigation, so there's no need to take a statement from Agent Lennix. From here on, LAPD will operate under our command. Load all seized evidence into the Bureau's vehicles."

The FBI agents brushed off Haig's reply and began ordering the officers to load the evidence into their vehicles. Haig watched with mounting irritation, while guilt welled up in Yuuto.

"I'm sorry," he said quietly. "The LAPD prevented the incident before anyone was hurt."

"There's nothing to be done. You can't go against the federal government." Haig patted Yuuto's arm before walking away. "Let's just be glad there were no casualties."

CHAPTER 12

The evening after the bomb scare, Yuuto received a call from Neto. He said he had something to discuss and asked to meet alone. So, after sunset, Yuuto headed downtown by himself.

The Mexican bar where they were supposed to meet was located on a relatively safe street, with a good mix of Chicanos, Whites, and Blacks. As Yuuto walked through the place, watching the patrons playing darts and looking for Neto, he saw Pepe—the man he'd met yesterday—coming toward him from down the hall.

"If you're looking for Neto, he's already here. This way."

Pepe led him to a booth at the very back of the bar, separated by a curtain. When Pepe called out, the curtain opened, and another man peeked out. He looked at Yuuto, then nodded for him to come inside.

On the sofa inside, Neto greeted Yuuto with a smile. "Sorry for dragging you out here on short notice," he said. "The neighborhood where I live can get dangerous at night, and I didn't want you going there alone."

"I appreciate the concern, but you make it sound like I'm some kind of sheltered princess," Yuuto replied as he sat across from him.

"Don't say that," Neto let out a chuckle of mild exasperation. "Last night, a cop got shot just down the street from my place. Want a drink? How about some tequila?"

"No, I'm driving," Yuuto said. "Anyway, what's this about? Did you find anything on *Ara Roja*?"

Neto told his two men to leave, and once they were gone, he finally started talking. "Thanks to Alonso pulling some strings, I was able to talk directly to one of the guy's cousins. I got the name of the supplier who was moving the product to *Ara Roja* back then."

Yuuto's expression lit up. "Tell me."

"First, look at this." Neto's face tightened as he opened a newspaper on the table. He tapped a section with his finger. "Here."

The article reported that a man named Jim Faber was shot and killed in the middle of the night on a street in Compton.

"And what about it?" Yuuto asked.

"This Faber guy was the one who supplied *Ara Roja* with massive shipments of cocaine."

Yuuto froze. After finally finding someone connected to White Heaven, he was too late—just one step behind, and the trail had gone cold. But as he buried his head in his hands, Neto said something strange.

"I'd known about Faber for a long time," Neto said. "In the underworld, he was a well-known drug dealer. But I didn't know he was dealing with *Ara Roja*. Back then, I was still locked up. I didn't have eyes on what was happening outside. So when I found out the guy you were looking for was the same guy Dick was after, I was honestly shocked."

Yuuto frowned, confused by Neto's words. "I don't get it. What does Dick have to do with this?"

"Yesterday, Dick came to me asking about Faber."

"Wait. Why the hell would Dick be asking about Faber?"

"I don't know the reason," Neto admitted. "When I was still behind bars, Dick called me using a fake name. He said he was looking for a man named Faber and wanted me to track him down. I was about to get out, so I promised him I'd look once I was free and gave him my contact information."

Yuuto's head spun. He didn't know how to make sense of any of this. "So you're saying Dick got Faber's location from you, and that same night, Faber just happened to get killed. That's what you're saying?"

"You think that's a coincidence?" There was a shadow in Neto's eyes.

"No way…" Yuuto shook his head. "Are you saying you think Dick killed Faber?"

"Doesn't that make the most sense?"

The words hit Yuuto like a blow. But as much as he didn't want to admit it, Neto was right. The timing was just too perfect.

Dick had killed someone.

Why?

Was it because Faber had been part of White Heaven? Was it some kind of revenge? Was Dick's target not just Corvus after all?

"I went back and forth on whether to tell you this," Neto said quietly. "I'd be breaking my word to Dick by saying anything. But I'm worried about him, Yuuto. What the hell is he planning to do?"

Yuuto couldn't answer.

"Yuuto," Neto continued, "I don't know what you and Dick are caught up in, but I do know you're in similar circumstances. I think you're the only one who can keep him from going over the edge."

Yuuto shook his head like a broken doll. "I can't. To Dick, I'm just a piece of his past he already threw away. Yesterday, he saw me and he ran. He didn't want to see me."

At last, he couldn't hold back. The feelings he had been suppressing came pouring out. When Yuuto lowered his gaze to his hand on the table, he noticed a small cut from the explosion the day before. It still throbbed faintly, but in a few days, the pain would fade.

The wound in his heart, though—the one left by seeing Dick and being avoided—would not heal so easily.

"When Dick got out of prison," Yuuto said softly. "He told me to forget him. Said it was for my own good. But I can't. If I could forget him, I would. God, I want to, but I can't stop worrying about him. When I think about him, I just…I can't sit still."

Neto's large hand settled over Yuuto's, warm and steady like an anchor. "Do you really care about Dick that much?"

It was a question that could have meant anything, but Yuuto knew Neto understood. Of course he did. Neto was too sharp not to.

"Is it really that obvious?" Yuuto gave a weak laugh. "Even Rob noticed."

"You let your guard down," Neto said with a faint smile. "That Rob guy might act easygoing, but he's got sharp eyes… Still, he's a good man."

"I think so too. I'm glad I met him."

"Then be grateful for good encounters," Neto said. "If you are, you'll keep having them. Meeting the right people…that's the best fortune anyone can have."

"I've been thinking this for a while, but you sound like a teacher sometimes."

"Go ahead, say it," Neto chuckled. "You really want to say that I sound preachy, don't you?"

"Maybe a little." Yuuto hesitated for just a second before blurting out, "But isn't it weird? For me to feel this way…about another guy?"

"There's nothing weird about loving someone," Neto said simply.

"But Rob says I might be wrong about how I feel."

"Wrong? What do you mean?"

Yuuto explained what Rob had told him, and Neto listened with keen interest.

"The suspension bridge effect, huh? Trust an academic to analyze love like it's a lab experiment," Neto said with a wry grin. "Sounds convincing, but not everything about the human heart can be reduced to data—especially love. You can dissect it all you want, but once you really fall for someone, the reasons stop mattering. If logic could stop your feelings, then they were never real to begin with."

The intensity in Neto's voice caught Yuuto off guard.

"You've...experienced a love you couldn't stop yourself from feeling, haven't you?"

"Of course I have," Neto replied with a faint laugh. "I've fallen for somebody even when I knew it was a bad idea, and I suffered for it."

Yuuto stared at him in surprise. He couldn't picture Neto—calm, collected Neto—getting so emotional over love. "But...they were all women, right?"

"Mostly," Neto admitted. "But once, I was drawn to a man. It was back when I was inside."

"You? Seriously? Was it just because there weren't any women around?"

Neto remained silent, his gaze fixed on Yuuto's hand, which he still held. His expression was calm, but there was a heaviness in the air that prompted Yuuto to quickly add, "It's okay. You don't have to tell me. I'm not trying to push."

"No," Neto said softly. "It's not that I don't want to talk about it. It's just...I don't know how to put it into words. No matter how I explain it, it never feels quite right."

He finally let go of Yuuto's hand and lifted his glass of tequila. "This was long before you ever came around. I met a young inmate—always in trouble, always picking fights like he had something to prove. He reminded me of a wounded animal, angry and defensive, and I couldn't just stand by," Neto recounted in a pained voice. "I tried to help, but he pushed me away at every turn. He trusted no one—least of all me. Still, I couldn't leave him alone. Even though I knew it was foolish, I continued to reach out. Little by little, after everything we went through, he began to open up to me. And then…"

Neto stopped, closed his eyes, and took a quick breath.

"He was stabbed. Right in front of me."

Yuuto stared silently at Neto, unable to speak. He thought he understood how dangerous prison was, but hearing it like this—learning that Neto had watched someone he cared about die—left him completely speechless.

"For what it's worth," Neto said quietly. "Dick helped me back then. I still don't fully understand him, but he's a man I trust. That hasn't changed. You feel the same way, don't you?"

Yuuto trusted Dick. Back in prison, Dick was the one person he could rely on. But now? Now he wasn't so sure. He didn't know what Dick was thinking or what he was planning. If Dick was rejecting him, maybe…maybe it was better to let him go.

"Yuuto," Neto said, his voice calm but steady. "The professor isn't entirely wrong, but you don't need to rush to figure it out. What matters isn't the reason or the timing—it's how you feel. If you still want to see Dick, then don't force yourself to give that up. Maybe, when you see him again, you'll finally understand what that feeling really is. Whether a love born on a suspension bridge turns out to be real, that's up to you."

Neto's words always had a way of grounding him. Every time Yuuto saw that unwavering strength in him, it made him want to be stronger as well.

"You really are like a teacher, Neto."

"I'd rather be your friend. I'll leave the lecturing to the

professor."

"Yeah…" Yuuto gave a small, tearful smile. "You're right."

CHAPTER 13

When Yuuto got home, Rob was lounging on the couch, reading a book with a glass of wine in hand.

"Welcome back," Rob said without looking up. "How was your date with Neto?"

Yuuto froze mid-step and frowned. "Could you not call it that? It makes it sound…I don't know. Improper."

"Oh, excuse me. Just a bit of jealousy, that's all. Don't mind me," Rob teased with a grin that could have been half-serious.

When Yuuto sat down next to him, Rob poured another glass and handed it to him.

"Here. You'll want one too."

"Thanks."

"So? Did you find anything from Neto?"

"Yeah," Yuuto answered. But he didn't say anything more right away.

Rob glanced up from his book. "Bad news? You've got that look."

There was no point in remaining silent. Yuuto took a breath and told Rob everything Neto had shared with him. As the story continued, Rob's expression grew increasingly grim.

"I see," he said at last. "If that's true, then I don't blame you for looking like hell."

Yuuto stared into his wine, his voice quiet. "Rob, what do you think justice is?"

Rob blinked, taken aback. “That’s a heavy question to spring on me out of nowhere.”

“I’ve lived my whole life by the law,” Yuuto said. “I even worked to uphold it, to catch criminals. And still, I was thrown into prison for something I didn’t do. If they hadn’t caught the real culprit, I’d still be rotting in there. Locked up, I lost faith in the whole damn idea of justice. I thought…maybe it doesn’t even exist. I raged against the law, wondering what the point of it all was.”

Yuuto gripped the glass tighter as he spoke.

“And Dick…Dick’s no different. He used to be in a special forces unit. I’m sure he’s killed people on missions before. But none of that is punished. Why?” Yuuto said quietly, his voice tight. “Because it was his job? Because it was for his country? It doesn’t change the fact that he took lives. And yet, what counts as a crime seems to shift depending on the situation. Isn’t it wrong to forgive every sin from the past, but condemn only the ones committed in the present?”

He didn’t believe what Dick had done was right. But no matter how hard he tried, he couldn’t condemn him. He didn’t want to.

“That’s a dangerous way of thinking,” Rob murmured under his breath, almost as if talking to himself.

“Huh?” Yuuto asked him with a confused look.

“Nothing. Forget it.” Rob just shook his head, put his glass down, and leaned back on the couch. “If you ask me what justice really is, I can’t give you a clear answer either. But there’s one thing I do know: there’s no such thing as absolute justice or absolute sin. That’s why we have laws. We decide on the rules we need, and we live by them. Sure, laws are imperfect. They always have been. But society needs order. Without it, imagine what the world would look like—no laws, no punishments. It’d fall apart overnight.”

“Yeah. You’re probably right,” Yuuto said quietly.

But deep down, he believed Rob could never truly understand. Rob didn't know what it was like to be betrayed by the very laws meant to protect you. He'd never been stripped of his freedom or had his life nearly ruined by a crime he didn't commit.

Only someone who had been through that could truly understand. Still, Yuuto didn't blame him. It wasn't Rob's fault.

"Yesterday's incident," Rob said abruptly, glancing at the TV. The news had been showing nonstop coverage of the bombing at San Gabriel Cemetery and the thwarted attack on the Japanese American National Museum since yesterday.

After a while, the program switched to politics. The screen displayed the Democratic presidential candidate campaigning in San Francisco.

"Looks like the election's heating up," Rob said.

It was an election year. The primaries and national conventions were over, and both the Republican and Democratic parties had officially chosen their candidates. Now the campaigns were in full swing—nationwide tours, televised debates, and nonstop coverage building toward the November general election.

"The Republican VP pick is Bill Manning, huh? Interesting choice."

The vice-presidential candidate was typically chosen by the party's presidential nominee at the national convention. If the nominee won the presidency, their selected running mate would automatically become vice president.

"Manning's the current White House Chief of Staff, isn't he?"

"Yeah. The man's a powerhouse." Rob nodded. "The president trusts him completely—hell, they say he's had enough influence to shape entire policies. He's been out of the spotlight until now, but maybe they're changing tactics."

When the news shifted to coverage of an international summit scheduled for New York at the end of next month, where major world leaders would gather, Rob picked up the remote and turned off the TV.

"Yuuto," Rob said, his voice thoughtful. "I've been thinking about something. Those words Dick left you with—'about the darkness festering in this place, that's where you'll find Corvus'"

"Yeah. Did you figure something out?"

"Only a theory," Rob cautioned. "But hear me out. Corvus told the former warden, Corning, that releasing Neto would, in the long run, be beneficial to the prison, right? However, in reality, a riot broke out, and the prison suffered extensive damage. That's a direct contradiction. But…if you think about it, a large-scale riot in a maximum-security prison would force a complete review of the security system. That would lead to tighter surveillance, remote-controlled tear gas systems, and other cutting-edge security upgrades."

"When we visited Schelger Prison, I noticed many new security cameras and advanced metal detectors—things that seemed to have been installed after the riot."

Yuuto leaned forward. "You're saying Corvus wanted the riot to happen—because the prison would profit from it?"

"That's right," Rob said. "And not just Schelger—other prisons would follow. If that happens, Smith-Bucks Company, which not only runs the prisons but also profits from security tech, would rake in astronomical sums. Their stock prices would skyrocket."

"Then—" Yuuto's eyes widened. "Corvus wasn't just tied to Corning; he's connected to Smith-Bucks itself! That has to be it, Rob—that's why Corvus could call me. That's how he knew I'd joined the FBI!"

Yuuto's voice rose with excitement, and Rob looked at him in surprise. "Call? You mean yesterday's call?"

"Yeah. I just got this phone recently, and only a few people have the number. I couldn't figure out how Corvus knew it. But now it makes sense. He got it from Carter."

"Carter…the new warden at Schelger?" Rob's brow furrowed, then he nodded. "Yeah, I see it. When the FBI showed up about Nathan, Carter must've panicked and called the company. And that information trickled straight to Corvus."

"Nathan's probably being sheltered by Smith-Bucks," Yuuto said, his voice rising with urgency. "This is huge, Rob. I need to call Heiden right now."

Yuuto pulled out his phone, but before he could dial, Rob muttered, his face dark with unease, "But terrorists working hand in hand with a corporation? What the hell does that even mean?"

"I don't know," Yuuto admitted. "But at least now we've got a target. If we dig into Smith-Bucks, we'll find something. And Rob… thanks. I feel like I'm one step closer to Corvus because of you."

Yuuto pressed the call button and brought up Heiden's number.

CHAPTER 14

"When we get there, I'm gonna take you to a great seafood place," Rob said, his tone light and almost boyish with excitement. For him, who had lived in D.C., it probably felt a little like going home.

"I'm looking forward to it," Yuuto replied.

The two of them were on a flight to Washington, D.C. They had been called back on short notice to meet Jack Eagan, the president of Smith-Bucks Company. To Yuuto's surprise, Rob was the one who arranged the meeting.

"I managed to get an appointment with the president," Rob had said. "Why don't you come with me?"

Rob had apparently requested the interview in his capacity as a university professor who studied the prison industry from an academic perspective—and, surprisingly, Eagan had agreed.

If Yuuto went in as an FBI agent, he risked alerting their target and pushing Corvus even deeper underground. But if he disguised himself as Rob's assistant, no one would bat an eye. After getting Heiden's okay, Yuuto packed his things and headed to D.C. with Rob.

"Those are the places where the string of bombings happened?" Rob asked now, leaning over from the seat next to him to peer at Yuuto's hands.

Yuuto was holding a U.S. map, its surface dotted with small black marks from a permanent marker. "Yeah. Something Corvus said on the phone keeps bothering me."

'Alpha' was meant to be the finale, but for you, I'll leave a special mark in L.A. too. Those words had been stuck in Yuuto's mind ever since.

"Yeah, that is strange," Rob admitted. "If L.A. was special, that means the other locations were chosen from the start."

Yuuto nodded. The two of them kept their voices low. "Exactly. Which means the previous bombing sites must mean something. If we can figure that out, maybe we can pinpoint the next one—he called it 'alpha,' remember? That has to be a clue."

"Hold on," Rob murmured, reaching for a pen. "Let me try something."

He drew four points—Michigan, Florida, Montana, and Utah—with precise ink strokes. The result was a skewed, stretched trapezoid.

"Huh. That leaves Arizona sitting just below Utah, all alone. I thought it might create a shape or something useful, but...nope."

Yuuto stared hard at the odd trapezoid Rob had drawn, then at the single point sitting just below it."I've seen this shape before."

Rob's head snapped toward him, his expression sharp with surprise. "Where?"

"I don't know. But I've seen it before… Damn it! I can't remember. What is it? I swear I've seen it somewhere." Yuuto raked his fingers through his hair in frustration. "Ugh, I hate it when this happens."

Rob gently patted his arm, as if trying to soothe him. "It'll come to you. Sometimes these things just click."

"Yeah, you're right." Yuuto forced himself to swallow his irritation and pushed the feeling down.

Just as he closed the file, the seatbelt sign lit up and the cabin announcement informed them that they were about to start their descent.

When they landed at National Airport, the two of them

headed directly to the FBI headquarters. Heiden greeted Rob with a noticeably restrained tone, avoiding his usual sarcastic edge. Although his thanks for Rob's cooperation were brief, he emphasized one point: the absolute need for confidentiality about anything they learned during the investigation.

After that, Heiden delivered some good news.

They had obtained a personnel list from the military camp, MSC, where Nathan had once been stationed. If Corvus's name showed up on it, it could finally give them a real lead on his true identity.

"We're going through every single name on that list," Heiden said. "With any luck, it'll lead us to Corvus. Oh, and one more thing—Smith-Bucks Company? Their actual parent company is General Mars."

"General Mars? The one that makes ships and aircraft?" Yuuto asked in surprise. Everyone in the United States was familiar with that name. It was one of the biggest heavy machinery manufacturers in the country.

"Yeah, that's the side most people know," Heiden replied. "But the real money comes from their defense division—fighter jets, military transports, satellites, missiles, warships. You name it, they sell it. Smith-Bucks was originally founded with funding from one of its subsidiaries. After a series of name changes, most people stopped noticing the connection."

After Heiden finished his explanation, Rob added, "The military-industrial complex and the prison-industrial complex share the same structure. Both are tangled knots of corporate and government interests. After the Cold War ended and military budgets were slashed, many defense contractors moved into the prison business."

"So when they ran out of enemies," Yuuto said. "They found a new one: crime."

"Exactly," Heiden interrupted, his tone sharp and eager to emphasize the point. "And that's why you need to be careful when you meet Jack Eagan, the president of Smith-Bucks. General Mars is closely connected to the government. If you stir things up with him, this investigation could be buried under political pressure so quickly you wouldn't even see it coming."

Yuuto straightened up, his expression becoming more serious. His meeting with Jack Eagan was set for tomorrow afternoon. Whatever happens, Eagan must not discover that Yuuto is with the FBI.

After parting ways with Heiden and leaving FBI headquarters, Yuuto and Rob went to their hotel. At the front desk, they checked in, only to find there were no single rooms available. They ended up with two twin room.

"We're meeting Eagan at a hotel near the White House," Rob said as they rode the elevator. "It's his usual spot whenever he's in D.C."

Smith-Bucks's headquarters might have been in New York, but Rob said Eagan often came to Washington—mostly to cozy up to politicians. Considering his work with government contracts, it made sense that he would constantly try to strengthen those connections.

"Do you actually know Eagan?" Yuuto asked.

"Back when I was at Georgetown, I ran into him a few times at parties. He appears like a polished gentleman, but when it comes to business, he's ruthless. He even offered me some tempting deals once, back when I was speaking out against prison privatization."

"Then isn't he going to be on guard tomorrow?"

"I'll keep it light," Rob said. "Safe questions only. The goal is not to piss him off."

Yuuto sank into a chair, frowning thoughtfully. That kind of interview would only skim the surface. A chance to sit with someone like Eagan was too valuable to waste on small talk.

"If we can get him comfortable," Yuuto said slowly, "we might be able to hit him with something unexpected at the end and see how he reacts."

Rob grinned. "Now that's a plan."

The two of them spent a while hashing out their strategy, carefully laying out how they'd steer the conversation. Once they had a rough outline, Rob suggested they grab dinner.

He took Yuuto to a seafood restaurant about ten minutes away by taxi. It wasn't fancy—in fact, it had a relaxed, no-frills vibe. Locals packed around the tables, eating while football played on the TVs mounted on the walls.

"If you don't have any picky preferences, leave the ordering to me," Rob said.

Yuuto shrugged and let him go. A little while later, their table was covered with platters of raw oysters, steamed crabs, crab cakes, and clam chowder.

"You think we can eat all this?" Yuuto asked, eyeing the spread.

"Don't worry," Rob said, cracking a crab claw with effortless skill. "These are Chesapeake Bay blue crabs—the best you'll ever have. Forget the Smithsonian. If you come to D.C., the first thing you should do is eat seafood."

As much as Rob had hyped it up, the food actually lived up to expectations. The local Foggy Bottom beer was surprisingly good, so good that Yuuto wondered why he'd never heard of it before.

Yuuto drank more than he probably should have, but Rob was a tank. Before long, Rob had started a conversation with the guy at the next table, gesturing animatedly while they debated the skill of some quarterback on the TV screen.

Just like Rob had said, there wasn't a single scrap of food left. Every dish had been neatly finished between the two of them. Full and satisfied, they headed back to the hotel and took turns with the shower.

When Yuuto, freshly showered, was lying on his bed watching the news, Rob emerged from the bathroom in a bathrobe, humming happily. He was clearly in a great mood. After all, he had enjoyed delicious food, and his favorite team had won.

"You're a strange guy," Yuuto said with a small smile. "I envy you."

"Huh? Envy me?" Rob, still toweling his hair dry, froze mid-motion and looked at him with surprise.

"You're always upbeat, get along with everyone, and seem to genuinely enjoy life."

Rob laughed and sat down on his bed. "What's with the sudden confession?"

"When I look at you, I can't help but feel like I'm missing something. I keep people at arm's length, and because of that, I rarely get close to anyone. Sometimes I feel like I'm just making my own world smaller."

"I don't see it that way. Sure, you're a little shy at first. But you really know how to connect with people. It might take longer, but that's not a flaw, it's just who you are," Rob said lightly, leaning back with a grin. "You like playing catch, Yuuto? I love it—throwing, catching, the whole thing."

"Catch?" Yuuto tilted his head. "That's a metaphor for something, isn't it?"

"Exactly. Playing catch is just like human relationships. Nothing starts unless you throw the ball, and it only keeps going if the other person throws it back. But it's not enough to just throw. If you throw wildly, you'll only piss the other person off. If they throw something impossible to catch, you get frustrated. You have to throw it right—where it actually reaches them."

"So it only works if both people put in the effort?"

"Bingo. Especially in love. At first, all you see is the other person's glove, and all you want to do is land the ball right in it. When it works, it feels amazing, and you're happier than you've ever been. But after a while, you stop paying attention. You get careless, and the whole thing stops being fun. And if one person stops throwing altogether, it's over. Throwing a ball to someone who won't catch it…there's nothing lonelier than that."

Yuuto gave him a small, amused smile. "That from personal experience?"

"You don't pull any punches, do you?" Rob chuckled wryly. "But yeah. I think whether a relationship lasts or not comes down to how much compassion you've got for the other person. Infatuation fades—if that's all you're running on, you're screwed. What really matters is whether you want to keep playing catch with that person, even when the thrill's gone."

"Yeah, that makes sense," Yuuto said. "People, love—if you overthink it, it just gets messy. But if you picture it as a simple game of catch…I get it."

"Right?" Rob smirked. "For the record, my last boyfriend stopped throwing the ball back about three months before we broke up. I kept throwing anyway, hoping he'd pick it up again…but he didn't. Turns out he was too busy playing catch with someone else."

Rob spoke in a light, easy voice, as if he'd long since left the past behind. But for Yuuto, listening to him stirred an uncomfortable pang in his chest.

"He's probably regretting it now," Yuuto muttered. "Cheating on the best boyfriend he could have had, that's just insane."

Rob chuckled. "I appreciate the compliment, but you've got to watch out for people who look perfect at first glance. Nobody's flawless. Usually, it just means they're really good at hiding their flaws."

"What about you then?" Yuuto asked. "What's your flaw,

Rob?"

Rob tilted his head, pretending to think. "If I had to pick one… maybe my flaw is that I don't have any."

"Oh, please," Yuuto said with a touch of sarcasm. "I can think of one flaw you have."

"Oh? And what's that? I can't imagine any."

"The way you twist logic to confuse people—then shamelessly pressure them for a kiss."

"You're still holding a grudge over that? Not my fault. Blame yourself for being too damn irresistible." Rob grinned without shame. "You're elegant, pretty, sexy—ridiculously charming. You really should realize the danger you cause."

Rob's face was deadly serious as he said it, which only made Yuuto burst out laughing until he doubled over.

"What the hell, Rob? All you did was spout a string of corny adjectives."

Yuuto tilted his head, curious at Rob's serious gaze.

"What?" Yuuto asked, tilting his head.

"You know," Rob murmured, "you're usually so cool, but when you laugh like that, you're adorable. It makes me want to crawl right into that bed of yours."

Yuuto immediately stopped laughing, narrowing his eyes in warning.

"I should warn you," he said dryly. "I have a black belt in karate. Try me, and you'll be the one to get hurt."

"If you're scared of getting hurt, you'll never fall in love," Rob replied with a lopsided grin.

And then he truly moved, crossing the space between their beds and sitting down beside Yuuto, his gaze gentle yet intense.

"Yuuto," he said softly, "can you really not see me that way? Not even a little?"

"Rob. Are you serious right now?"

"I am. I like you. We may not have known each other for long, but I swear to you, this feeling is real."

Faced with such a straightforward confession, Yuuto couldn't dodge the truth. "I like you too," he admitted. "But only as a friend. I-I can't think about anyone but Dick right now. I'm sorry, Rob. I can't be your boyfriend."

"Yeah. I figured. I guess I can't compete with Dick, huh?" Rob lowered his gaze and nodded once. "But if I catch you with your guard down, you don't mind if I try hitting on you again, right? You'd at least let me have that much, wouldn't you?"

He truly was the kind of man who refused to walk away empty-handed. Yuuto offered a wry smile and shook his head.

"You're unbelievable, you know that?"

"Well, no one likes a guy who can't take no for an answer," Rob smirked. "I'll accept my rejection and slink off to bed with my tail between my legs. Good night."

He pulled the sheets over his head in mock offense, and Yuuto had to hold back a laugh as he turned off the lights.

Even after he closed his eyes, Yuuto kept thinking about what Rob had said. His feelings for Dick were…complicated. They didn't fit neatly into the boxes that experience and common sense said they should. But maybe Rob was right. Maybe if he thought of it as just a game of catch, it wouldn't feel so heavy.

It was the labels—love, friendship, sympathy—that haunted him. He kept trying to force his feelings into one category or another, only to find none of them fit—all that endless overthinking…just to reassure himself of something.

But the truth was simple.

He wanted to throw a ball to Dick. He wanted Dick to catch it. And when Dick threw it back, Yuuto wanted to be the one to catch it.

Not anyone else.

Not Rob.

Not anyone.

Only Dick.

That was Yuuto's one, undeniable wish.

CHAPTER 15

The following afternoon, the hotel where Jack Eagan was staying was just three blocks from the White House. It was an upscale, European-style hotel with a refined atmosphere. However, given its proximity to the White House, the lobby was crowded with businessmen in dark suits, all of whom seemed to belong in a boardroom.

Eagan's suite was on the top floor. Yuuto and Rob were led into the living room by a man who was probably his secretary. After a few minutes of waiting on the sofa, Eagan came out of the adjoining room, walking toward them confidently.

He appeared to be in his late forties, though Rob had told Yuuto he was actually fifty-three. And, just as Rob described, he had the polished look of a gentleman—handsome, composed, and unmistakably sharp.

"Sorry to keep you waiting. Dr. Connors, it's been a while," Eagan said smoothly.

"Thank you so much for agreeing to this on such short notice," Rob said, shaking hands before gesturing toward Yuuto.

"And this is?"

"This is my assistant, Alan Chen. He's young, but incredibly capable," Rob said with an easy smile, lying through his teeth.

Yuuto offered a polite greeting of his own and extended his hand. "A pleasure to meet you."

Eagan didn't seem suspicious at all. He shook Yuuto's hand and then motioned for them to sit down.

"Shall we get started right away?" Rob asked. "I wouldn't want to waste a busy man's time."

At Rob's cue, Yuuto set a voice recorder on the table and pulled out a notepad, scribbling in it to seem engaged.

"As you know, Mr. Eagan," Rob began smoothly. "I've long been skeptical about privatizing prisons, advocating for caution. But given the current reality, it's clear that private prisons are now deeply embedded in the global capitalist system and have become an essential part of modern American society. With that in mind, could you share your company's philosophy as an organization entrusted with public responsibility?"

Eagan offered a practiced smile. "Of course. We see ourselves as more than just a business. We take pride in fulfilling a vital mission of social service. After all, eradicating crime from society entirely is impossible. What we can do is help rehabilitate offenders and prepare them for their return to society—"

While Yuuto pretended to take notes carefully, deep inside, he couldn't shake his disappointment. Eagan's words were just a shiny facade. In Yuuto's experience, nothing in prison life seemed to offer rehabilitation or a hopeful way back into society.

Rob played along, nodding now and then with a casual, "That's impressive," or "Well said," offering just enough praise to keep Eagan comfortable. Pleased with himself, Eagan went on answering questions for nearly an hour.

Finally, Rob let out a satisfied sigh, as if their discussion had come to an end.

"This has been incredibly insightful. Your perspective is outstanding, Mr. Eagan. I believe I might need to reevaluate my stance on the privatization of prisons."

"I'm very glad to hear it," Eagan replied warmly. "If promising young scholars like Dr. Connors see the value of our work, it only strengthens our position."

Just then, Eagan's secretary came in with fresh coffee. As the atmosphere lightened, Rob struck up a casual conversation. Then, with calculated ease, he added, "Oh, that reminds me. Not long ago, there was a riot at Schelger Prison in California, wasn't there? I hear Smith-Bucks Company runs that facility for the state. The repairs and renovations must have been quite the challenge."

Eagan sighed in clear frustration. "They were. The racial tensions inside the prison are an ongoing problem that can't be easily solved. Strengthening security measures is one of our top priorities."

"I also heard two inmates escaped during that riot," Rob continued. "They still haven't been caught, have they?"

"A troubling matter," Eagan said sharply, face darkened. "I can't imagine what the police are doing."

"Speaking of the police," Rob said lightly. "I've got some friends in the LAPD who passed along an interesting rumor. One of the escapees—Nathan Clark, if I recall—was said to have been helped by none other than Schelger Prison's former warden, Mr. Corning. And he's the one who turned up dead recently, isn't he? What's your take on that, Mr. Eagan?"

For the first time, Eagan's expression hardened.

"Who's been spreading such baseless nonsense?" he demanded.

"Well," Rob replied smoothly, "The police seem to believe that Clark himself killed Mr. Corning."

"If that was true, then Corning must have felt threatened by that inmate and was forced to help him escape. He was a diligent, upright man. There was no way he would have taken a prisoner out on his own. I've known him for a long time, so I can say that with absolute certainty. He was a man I could truly trust. That's why, ever since Corning disappeared, I haven't stopped worrying. I was convinced he must have been caught up in some kind of incident."

"I see."

"If the interview's over, I'll take my leave now. I have another appointment to keep." Although his expression stayed friendly, his attitude had clearly hardened. Rob and Yuuto thanked him, then left Eagan's office.

"How'd it go?" Rob asked Yuuto as they walked down the hallway.

"That last thing he said stuck with me. He claims to believe in Corning, but while Corning's been missing, he went ahead and brought in Carter as the new warden. If he trusted Corning that much, wouldn't he at least wait until he confirmed whether he was alive or dead before making any personnel changes?"

"Good point. Maybe he knew from the beginning that Corning wasn't coming back," Rob said as they stepped into the elevator.

"And if he truly decided to protect Corvus even after one of his valued employees was killed…that's insane. What exactly is Corvus to that company?"

"No idea. But one thing's clear: it's worth a hell of a lot more to them than human life."

The elevator arrived on the first floor, and the two of them stepped out, crossing the lobby under a glittering chandelier. It was just as they passed the front desk that Yuuto's eyes locked onto the back of a man checking in.

He was tall, wearing a sharp suit, with broad shoulders and long legs that caught the eye at a glance.

"Yuuto?" Rob looked at him with a puzzled expression when Yuuto suddenly stopped dead in his tracks.

"Thank you for waiting, Mr. Müller. Your room is eight-oh-nine. One of our staff will be happy to escort you—"

"That won't be necessary. Just give me the key," a low voice cut off the receptionist's polite words.

Yuuto froze, staring at the man's back, his breath momentarily forgotten as a wave of pure shock ran through him.

He can't be here. It's impossible. It's just someone who looks like him. He told himself that over and over, but he still couldn't tear his gaze away.

The man took the key, lifted the bag he'd set beside his feet, and turned. The moment he shifted, his sharply defined profile came into view—

A high, sharp nose bridge. Cool, clear eyes. A well-shaped jawline.

It was, without a doubt, Dick Burnford standing right there. There was no way Yuuto could have mistaken him at such close range. Seeing Dick in front of him made Yuuto's heart pound wildly, his chest tightening with disbelief.

It felt like he was trapped in a dream.

"Yuuto, what's wrong?"

Dick turned at Rob's voice, and their eyes met instantly.

Dick's blue eyes remained fixed on Yuuto, but his expression didn't flicker in the slightest. Instead of looking at a stranger, it was as if no one was there at all—a perfect, unreadable poker face.

Just like when Yuuto saw him in front of Neto's house, Dick's hair was a dark brown. It was much shorter now, neatly combed, and the silver-framed glasses he wore gave him an entirely different vibe from the Dick who'd been in prison.

In summary, he exuded the presence of a sharp, capable businessman with abundant intelligence. The most surprising change was that the large scar running from his forehead to the edge of his eyebrow had completely vanished.

"Steve, are you done checking in yet?" A slender blonde woman appeared from behind Dick. She appeared to be in her mid-thirties, heavily made up, but with a distinctly sharp and intelligent beauty.

"Yeah. Sorry to keep you waiting," Dick replied softly. The woman smiled charmingly, looping her arm through his.

"Oh, could it be...*Rob?*" The woman's eyes widened in surprise the moment she saw Rob.

"Hey, Jessica. It's been a while," Rob said warmly. "Still as beautiful as ever."

"Ah, it's definitely Rob!"

Rob and Jessica embraced briefly, clearly delighted by the unexpected reunion. Yuuto could only stare in shock as it sank in—Rob knew Dick's companion.

"This is really surprising. Are you staying at this hotel?"

"No, I'm staying at the Madison Hotel. I came here to meet with President Eagan. I just finished interviewing him."

"Is that so? If you have time while you're in D.C., we should grab a meal together."

"It's a privilege to be invited by the most beautiful woman on K Street."

"You're the same as always. Call me anytime," she said before turning her gaze to Yuuto. "And this is?"

Rob quickly replied, "He's my assistant. This is Alan Chen. He assists with research. Alan, this is Jessica Foster. She's a savvy lobbyist contracted by Smith-Bucks Company."

Lobbyists focus on persuading politicians to enact laws and regulations that benefit their clients. Because Jessica was associated with Smith-Bucks, Rob intentionally introduced Yuuto under a false name.

While Yuuto and Jessica shook hands, Rob looked at Dick and asked, "So, is that charming fellow your boyfriend?"

"No way, nothing like that," Jessica denied, though her expression suggested otherwise.

"He's Steve Müller. He works at a systems development

company, and I brought him to meet President Eagan."

Steve Müller—that was the name Dick was using now.

Yuuto experienced a complex mix of emotions upon realizing Dick was once again disguised as someone else. Clearly, Dick was after Corvus and had contacted Smith-Bucks Company. For now, he had no option but to continue acting as another man.

"Steve, this is Rob Connors. He's young but a well-known criminologist in those fields."

"Müller." Dick gave Rob a formal handshake. "It's an honor to meet you."

Jessica glanced at her wristwatch and smiled apologetically. "I'm meeting with President Eagan now. Let's talk more another time."

"Definitely. I'll call you."

Jessica and Dick walked off toward the elevator hall.

"He's a good-looking guy," Rob remarked appreciatively, watching them go. "He's probably just trying to charm her so he can pitch his company's products to the president. Having a handsome face can be useful. Don't you think, Yuuto?"

"Yeah." Yuuto gave a distracted reply, his eyes fixed on Dick's retreating back.

CHAPTER 16

Yuuto and Rob chose to have an early dinner at the hotel restaurant.

During the meal, Rob discussed Jessica's talent as a lobbyist and mentioned that she was the niece of the company president. It was clear that getting close to her would make it easier to access inside information about Smith-Bucks Company. That was probably why Dick was targeting her. The systems development company was likely a front for the CIA.

After finishing their meal and just as they were about to go back to their rooms, Rob's phone rang. It appeared to be a call from a friend inviting him out.

"Eh? Now? Hmm…what should I do?"

"Why not? Go ahead," Yuuto said. "I'm a little tired, so I'll head up and rest."

Rob nodded, giving him an apologetic look before ending his call.

"Sorry," he said. "That was an old co-worker. He's with the rest of the gang and asked if I could join."

"Don't mind me. Go and have fun."

After seeing Rob off, Yuuto returned to their room alone. Fresh from the shower, a towel around his waist, he let himself drop onto the bed without even bothering to get dressed.

Finally reunited with Dick, but his heart felt anything but light. In fact, he felt more depressed than before seeing him.

Dick's cold eyes had struck Yuuto's heart hard. They were both wearing masks for the reunion; it couldn't be helped. Still, Yuuto had wished for just a single moment, even one second, to see some joy of reunion reflected in Dick's eyes. Just one second to feel like the old days, to be seen by him again.

Lying on his back, Yuuto stared blankly at the ceiling. Even with his eyes open, Dick's face appeared in his mind—cold and rejecting him.

Tossing and turning restlessly, Yuuto bit his lip to hold back the storm of intense emotions raging inside him.

I want to see him. I want to see Dick so badly.

If only they were somewhere alone, maybe they could go back to how things used to be, shed their masks, and enjoy a reunion. He remembered the room number. If he left now, he would still have time to see him.

Unable to stay still any longer, Yuuto put on his suit again and hurried out of his room. He flagged down a taxi in front of the hotel and told the driver the name of the hotel where Dick was staying.

A wave of anxiety and hope flickered in his chest, threatening to overwhelm him. But the moment Yuuto arrived at the hotel and entered the lobby, a sudden thought hit him—what if Dick was in the same room as Jessica? His feet froze. He couldn't just walk into the room without warning. If Jessica was there too, it would only raise questions.

After hesitating, Yuuto decided to call the hotel front desk from his cell phone and try to connect to Dick's room.

Just as he was about to step into a quiet corner of the lobby, someone grabbed his arm from behind. Startled, Yuuto turned around and gasped when he saw who it was.

"Dick—"

Dick looked down at him coldly, expressionless.

"Come."

With a brisk command, Dick walked away quickly, and Yuuto hurried to follow. Dick stepped into the elevator and immediately pressed the close door button. Without saying a word, they arrived on the eighth floor and started down a long hallway.

Dick opened the door to room 809 and looked back at Yuuto. When Yuuto hesitated, Dick roughly pushed him inside. The room had a queen bed, but there was no sign of any woman's belongings. Seeing that Dick was staying alone, Yuuto felt a wave of relief.

"Dick, sorry for coming so suddenly."

"Don't call me that. I'm Steve Müller now." His tone was cold and dismissive. "You're a nuisance when you hang around. Can't you understand that much?"

The anger radiating from Dick's entire body crushed Yuuto's hopes without mercy. Even when alone, Dick's attitude stayed cold. There was not a hint of joy or warmth in their reunion. Yuuto painfully realized he was already nothing more than a discarded memory to Dick.

He could no longer find the words to speak.

Coming here like this had been his desperate attempt to show his feelings: *I haven't forgotten you. I've always wanted to see you.*

Yet to Dick, it was nothing but a bother. It was a one-sided longing all along.

"What did you come here for?"

"What did I—?"

The ball Yuuto threw was never caught. It completely missed Dick's glove and just dropped, hitting his back. Dick didn't want to play catch with him. That was the one and only truth.

"Did you come here to keep an eye on me because someone higher up told you to?"

"Keep an eye on you?"

"I know you joined the FBI. You thought that by spying on me, you'd find out where Corvus was hiding, didn't you?"

Yuuto stared at Dick's sharp features in confusion. Was his coldness because Yuuto was now with the FBI? Because he had joined the opposing side?

"I did become an FBI agent. But it wasn't to oppose you. In fact, I wanted to see you again—"

"Don't make excuses. I shared information about Corvus hoping an innocent man like you could get out of prison. It wasn't meant to help the FBI. Yet as soon as you got out, you became their dog. You actually chose a job that interferes with me. It feels like a betrayal," Dick said bitterly, turning his face away from Yuuto as if he couldn't bear to look at someone he hated anymore.

"Dick, that's not true. I'm not trying to get in your way—"

"Then quit the FBI right now. If you can't, then get out of my sight. You're a nuisance."

The CIA and FBI were definitely at odds. One tried to assassinate Corvus, while the other desperately aimed to arrest him. Since they belonged to opposing agencies, it was only natural that Dick and Yuuto would also become enemies.

Yuuto understood that in his head, but he never thought it would affect their personal relationship. He never imagined Dick would despise him this much.

He cursed his own foolishness from the depths of his heart. He knew all too well how much Dick was driven by his pursuit of Corvus. Dick was risking everything to kill Corvus. Yuuto understood that perfectly.

He wanted to understand Dick, to be the person who understood him best. But in reality, he had only been thinking about his own feelings. That was the most embarrassing truth of all.

"I'm sorry. I was reckless. I joined the FBI thinking that if I chased Corvus, I'd see you again—that I could belong in your world. I thought it would be simple. But all I've done is cause you trouble…" His voice shook. Yuuto clenched his fists, fighting to hold back the storm of emotions raging inside him.

"Why did you want to see me?"

Yuuto was confused by Dick's question. Dick should already understand his feelings.

"Could it be that you can't forget that night we had sex?"

"Dick?"

"Was it really that good?" Dick stepped closer and grabbed Yuuto's chin roughly. "I'll admit, the sex was satisfying. You came on so coyly it put me in the mood—and it wasn't bad. The situation only made it more thrilling. If you're that desperate, I'll do you a favor and sleep with you once more. But it'll be the last time. Get your fill, and never come after me again."

Behind his glasses, Dick's blue eyes gazed down at Yuuto as if they were piercing him. Yuuto looked back in stunned silence.

His blood ran cold. His hands and feet went numb. It wasn't the shock of Dick's words that hurt—it was the painful truth that Dick was desperately trying to push him away.

No matter how much of a nuisance Yuuto was to Dick now, he hadn't expected him to ridicule that moment they shared. It was supposed to have been important. It wasn't just physical intimacy; they had also shared their hearts with each other. They had sought each other deeply, with their very souls.

"If you want it, go to bed. Let's get this over with."

That was enough. Yuuto couldn't bear to hear another word. Deep down, he knew he was the one allowing Dick to lash out. The cruelty was deliberate; Dick was using harsh words to cut their bond for good.

"What's wrong? Say something."

Yuuto gently pushed against Dick's chest. "It's fine now, Dick."

"What is?"

"I can tell you don't mean any of it. So please, just stop."

Dick twisted his lips into a mocking sneer. "How do you know I don't mean it? Don't say selfish things based on your assumptions."

"I know. Of course I know…" Yuuto shook his head hard, overwhelmed by the storm of emotions inside him. "If I'm such a nuisance, I won't come near you again. But…even if it's a lie, please don't belittle what happened that night. To me, it's still a precious memory. Even if you forget, I'll remember it for the rest of my life. I'll never forget."

Yuuto turned his back on Dick and slowly walked toward the exit. He didn't want to make him suffer anymore or force him to speak more cruel words. That was the only thought in his mind.

His hand hovered over the doorknob, and after hesitating, Yuuto spoke his last words.

"No matter where you are, I'll pray for your peace of mind. For your happiness."

A strong sense of déjà vu washed over Yuuto as he uttered the words. He had said the same thing when Dick escaped from prison. Back then, he saw Dick off with a faint smile. But now, he couldn't even manage a smile. He couldn't even bring himself to look at Dick's face.

Just as he painfully reached to open the door, a sudden, powerful impact hit his back.

For a moment, Yuuto didn't understand what had happened. Then, realizing Dick was holding him tightly from behind, the door in front of him blurred.

"Dick?"

Strong arms stopped him in his tracks. Trapped in a fierce embrace, he couldn't move.

"Dick, why—"

Tears streamed down Yuuto's face. Dick said nothing. Only ragged breaths brushed past his face. Suddenly, Dick spun him around and held him facing him. Wrapped in Dick's broad chest, Yuuto's tears flowed even more freely. He lifted his head to look at Dick's face, but Dick turned away, wearing a pained expression as if struggling to hold something back.

Stretching out his hand, Yuuto gently brushed Dick's cheek with his fingertips. At Yuuto's touch, Dick's body shook. Hesitating, Yuuto cupped Dick's face with both hands. Dick took a deep breath, eyes downcast, seemingly afraid to meet Yuuto's gaze.

"Dick, please look at me," he whispered softly, then took off Dick's glasses. With gentle fingers, he tousled Dick's neatly combed bangs. Somehow, it made the man before him seem to revert to the Dick he once knew.

"Please, look me in the eyes."

With that plea, Dick finally opened his eyes. Their breaths mingled as their eyes locked in an intense gaze. At the sight of those trembling blue eyes, Yuuto was sure: this was the Dick Burnford he had known at Schelger Prison. The same man from back then.

"Yuuto…you always break my heart. Why is that…?" Dick murmured, his voice barely audible as he traced Yuuto's face with trembling fingers. From his forehead to his temple, down the bridge of his nose to his lips—a hesitant touch, like someone blind confirming the presence of another. "When I see you, I know I'll lose my resolve. That's why I didn't want to meet you."

"Dick, don't you hate me?" Yuuto couldn't help but ask. He needed to know if Dick could ever forgive him for becoming an FBI agent.

"There's no way I could hate you. Even if you killed me, I wouldn't hate you."

A heat rose from deep within Yuuto's chest. It blossomed into joy and quickly spread through his entire body, bringing fresh tears to his eyes.

"Dick, I've wanted to see you all this time. Even after we parted ways, I couldn't stop thinking about you—what you were feeling, where you were, what you were doing. Again and again, nothing else filled my mind but you…"

When they had held each other at Schelger Prison, Yuuto felt as if a part of Dick's soul had merged with his own. It was an irrational, purely blind obsession that defied logic.

"I was the opposite. I tried not to think about you. When I did, my emotions spiraled out of control, and I couldn't move forward. I was desperately trying to forget you."

That meant Dick had felt the same way Yuuto did. It wasn't just Yuuto alone. They both shared this painful feeling, despite the distance between them.

Yuuto took Dick's hand and pressed his cheek against the large palm. Overjoyed by the warmth, he kissed Dick's hand again and again. Dick pulled him close, teasing his cheek and earlobe with hot lips.

Even without kissing, their breaths grew ragged. Wrapped in excitement and anticipation like the climax of a moment, they couldn't remain calm.

Dick pressed his hips firmly against Yuuto, the heat of desire unmistakable. The arousal straining beneath his pants made his intent clear. Yuuto felt it too—he wanted Dick with all his heart. And yet, he wasn't sure if he could truly surrender to those feelings.

Was it right to give in to desire now? Considering what lay ahead, maybe it was better to part ways without acting. It may be painful now, but it will be easier to handle later.

But they had finally met again. Dick was finally looking at him.

"Dick, what should I do?" Helpless with the heat flooding through his body, Yuuto asked plaintively. "What are we supposed to do now?"

"There's nothing left to do. Did you really think I'd just let you walk away?" Dick's smile was complex, a mix of resignation and passion—yet it was the first gentle expression he'd shown since their reunion. "Let's forget everything for now. Our positions, our work, and all the obligations awaiting us. Just forget it all—right here, right now."

Right now. Just this moment.

Even knowing it wouldn't last, Yuuto's heart ached.

It felt the same—as if nothing had changed since that time they had made love in prison. Their circumstances were different now, yet the scene was unchanged.

Were they destined to love each other only within stolen moments, bound by time and place? Were they forbidden from promising anything beyond the present?

"Do you hate it, Yuuto?"

Yuuto wanted to say yes. To say he hated it—that they only sought each other for now, to be torn apart again. That the thread that bound them would snap once more. He didn't want such a hollow relationship. But that was selfish. He had no right to block the path Dick was determined to walk.

With a helpless sigh, Yuuto laid his head against Dick's chest.

"Yuuto?"

"I can't go back either. I can't part with you feeling like this."

Dick lifted Yuuto forcefully. Yuuto's breath caught as he wrapped his arms tightly around Dick's neck.

Before he realized it, they were on the bed, Dick straddling him. Dick's heated tongue parted his lips and plunged deep, and Yuuto kissed back with desperation. Each fervent kiss was a sweet poison, spreading through him until his whole body tingled. Whatever reason he had left had already melted away.

No thought was necessary. Like animals guided by instinct, they searched for each other without hesitation. They abandoned everything else and surrendered to unrestrained desire.

Dick tore away Yuuto's clothes and began exploring the exposed skin with hot, hungry hands. Every touch sent waves of sweet ache through him. On the tangled, rumpled sheets, Yuuto trembled with bittersweet longing.

Dick roughly shed his own suit, pressing their bare skin together—the soft, moist contact intoxicated Yuuto, who clung to Dick's back in ecstasy.

"Dick…Dick…"

Each time he called out to him in delirium, the man answered with a kiss. Their erections pressed together, slick with arousal, precum smearing between them with every rub. Yet neither reached down to touch the other directly. Both held back, afraid that once they climaxed, this feverish tension would shatter.

With his legs spread wide, Yuuto felt Dick's fingers tracing along the insides of his thighs, teasing him from the base of his legs to his most sensitive places, over and over. At the same time, Dick's mouth alternated between the two peaks of his chest, licking and tasting. Yuuto bit back the moan that nearly escaped.

The frustrating sensation of fingertips almost touching but not quite was agonizing. The constant teasing of his chest, along with the heat intensifying between his legs, made Yuuto's desire spike even higher. He felt as if he might climax at any moment, despite having no direct stimulation.

His throbbing length ached unbearably, the tip burning with raw, searing heat, as if it were an open wound. Drenched to the root in his own slick arousal, Yuuto couldn't hold back any longer—he ground himself desperately against Dick's waist.

"Dick, I…can't…*Please!*"

Yuuto's hips lifted from the sheets, swaying them shamelessly as if to entice Dick. His body moved on its own, surrendering to desire beyond his control.

"Already close? Can't hold back?"

He answered Dick's whisper with a silent nod. Dick's fingers closed around Yuuto's slick shaft, and even the faintest stroke made him writhe in silent torment, trembling on the edge of release.

"I'm coming—"

"No. Not yet. Hold on a little longer." Dick shifted his body and brought his face between Yuto's legs. "I want to taste you first."

"Dick, no…hurry, let's—"

Yuuto's desperate plea for union went unanswered as Dick lost himself in the act. His grip tightened at the base, holding back release, while his mouth consumed Yuuto with a scorching heat that seared like a brand.

"Ah, no…!"

Each fervent pull of Dick's lips sent spasms through Yuuto's thighs. The mounting urge to climax made him try to push Dick's head away, but his hands were caught and pinned to the sheets.

Arching back, Yuuto shook his head in helpless denial, tears springing to his eyes as the almost-painful pleasure overwhelmed him. Trapped beneath Dick's relentless mouth, he could only release soft, desperate cries.

"No, Dick, please, not so rough—I can't!"

Though he didn't want to climax alone, Yuuto's body had slipped beyond his control, left utterly at the mercy of Dick's caresses.

He felt the tip of Dick's tongue pressing at his slit, felt himself swallowed deeper into that burning mouth. Even the wet, obscene sounds filled his ears, violating him further. Before he realized it, his hips were giving small, helpless thrusts in rhythm with Dick's movements. Shame burned through him, but he couldn't resist—the mingled waves of pleasure, humiliation, and raw arousal only dragged him closer to the brink.

"Ah…I can't hold on anymore…Dick…"

Dick finally loosened his hold at Yuuto's base. In an instant, Yuuto spilled into his mouth, the violent rush of pleasure so overwhelming it nearly made him black out. His mind went blank, his body collapsing in boneless surrender. Chest heaving, he drew in deep, ragged breaths, trembling with the aftershocks.

"Yuuto, not yet. The real thing starts now," Dick whispered against Yuuto's chest as he caressed it with a passionate rhythm.

A shiver ran down Yuuto's spine at the sound of Dick's low, desire-laden voice. When Dick's hand slid along his side, the searing touch was enough to stir him again, rekindling his arousal despite having climaxed only moments earlier.

"Let me do you, too." Yuuto reached out to Dick's still-hard cock, but was gently pushed back.

"We'll get to that later." Suddenly, Dick sat up and picked up the phone receiver. Yuuto held his breath and watched Dick's lips absentmindedly, curious about who he was calling. "I want to order a cheese pizza. And please send a bottle of olive oil. Yeah, thanks."

"Room service." After hanging up, Dick pressed his body back against Yuuto's. Yuuto smiled faintly, brushing a soft kiss over the tip of his nose, savoring the warmth of his closeness and the comforting weight against him.

"Getting a snack before the main event?"

"No way. I'm too busy savoring you to even think about eating."

"Then why order pizza?"

Dick affectionately tousled Yuuto's shiny black hair and let out a wry sigh. "God, you're impossible, stop being so cute. It's not the pizza I want. It's the oil."

Realizing Dick's true intent, Yuuto flushed, embarrassed by his own dullness.

"Oh."

"One bottle might not be enough." Teasing, Dick bit gently at Yuuto's earlobe. "I'll drench you in oil and savor every inch of you. Be ready."

"Dick…" Yuuto pushed at Dick's broad chest, squirming from the ticklish assault, but Dick didn't budge. Instead, he dug into Yuuto's ribs and teased his belly button, drawing gasps and helpless laughter as Yuuto thrashed across the bed, struggling to catch his breath.

"Stop it already…you idiot, Dick! Damn it…"

Overpowered by the difference in weight, Yuuto sank his teeth into Dick's bicep in frustrated defiance, leaving a set of teeth marks as his small act of rebellion.

"Hey, biting's cheating."

"So what? It's your fault, Dick." Yuuto shot back angrily.

"You really haven't changed." Dick rolled his eyes and raised one brow in exasperation. "Your stubbornness is legendary."

"And your mean streak isn't any better."

Yuuto let out a playful huff through his nose. Dick only shook his head with a helpless smile and drew him into a warm embrace.

"Let's call it even. I was the one at fault."

"Glad you realize that."

Dick was still crouched over Yuuto, his face buried in the pillow as he laughed. Yuuto couldn't help but join him, their laughter spilling together until it softened into a string of gentle kisses, traded again and again.

"I can finally make love to you in a clean bed…it feels like a dream."

Yuuto remembered then—how, after they'd had sex on a cardboard floor, Dick had sounded frustrated, saying he'd wanted their first time to be on a proper, well-made bed.

This brief happiness was precious. Because they both knew it was only temporary, Yuuto treasured it even more.

Once they left this room, they would be apart again. Even if they crossed paths somewhere, they would have to pretend to be strangers and pass each other by.

Pushing aside the ache rising in his chest, Yuuto threaded his fingers through Dick's hair. The dark color suited him, yet Yuuto still longed for the dazzling blond he once had—so much more.

"Your scar healed nicely."

Tracing the area on Dick's forehead, Yuuto saw a faint redness but hardly any sign of the old wound.

"After the prison break, they took me to a hospital because they didn't want me to have any noticeable marks."

"Dick, can I ask you one thing?" Yuuto's voice dropped.

Dick's expression darkened. "If it's about Corvus, I won't say a word."

I know, it's not that… It's Jessica. The woman you were with today." Yuuto hesitated, his voice faltering. "What's the deal with her? Are you…?"

"Are we what?" Dick's serious gaze locked onto Yuuto's.

Feeling awkward, Yuuto looked away. "I'm asking if you've already slept with her. You two seemed pretty close."

"What, are you jealous?"

"No…I mean—yeah, I am." Yuuto reluctantly admitted it, thinking denial would be obvious anyway.

"Not yet," Dick whispered, stroking Yuuto's hair. "But if

necessary, I'll do it. She's an important source of information."

"I see." Though uneasy inside, Yuuto maintained a calm front and played the part of an understanding man. He didn't mind if Dick knew he was jealous, but he couldn't afford to cause unnecessary fuss—he wasn't in that position.

"But," Dick murmured, burying his nose in the nape of Yuuto's neck with an amused expression. "I'll probably fail that mission. My little junior is no use against a woman."

Yuuto smiled, and Dick kissed his collarbone before turning the question back to him. "How about you? What's your relationship with that guy?"

"That guy? You mean Rob?"

"Yeah. Some renowned professor, huh? Doesn't matter—he still looked like a creep."

"That's a bit harsh. He's a good guy—he's helping me with the investigation. We only just met, but he's been really cooperative, and I'm genuinely grateful."

As Yuuto praised Rob, Dick's expression darkened. "But that guy's gay, right? Hasn't he hit on you?"

"How did you know?" Yuuto asked, surprised.

Dick's face grew even grumpier. "So he did come onto you."

"Not that. I mean, how did you figure out Rob was gay just by looking at him?"

"Just a feeling. The way he looked at Jessica was cold. A man who likes women would never look so distant in front of such beauty. No matter how much he tries to be a gentleman, he'd end up drooling."

Yuuto thought Rob's attitude was quite friendly, so he was genuinely surprised by Dick's sharp observation.

"But how do *you* know he's gay?" Dick asked, not letting the matter drop. "Did he just come out to you, the guy he just met?"

"Well…" Yuuto couldn't bring himself to admit that Rob had taken him to a gay bar—and even kissed him.

"So he made a move on you. Damn that bastard!" Dick sounded genuinely angry, which Yuuto found strange.

"Dick, are you jealous too? That doesn't seem like you."

"Why not? I might not look it, but I'm a jealous guy—you just don't realize it."

"You don't seem like the jealous type."

Trying to soothe the still-grumpy Dick, Yuuto intertwined his fingers with Dick's long ones.

"I was jealous even in prison."

"Jealous of *who*?" Yuuto burst out in surprise at the unexpected confession.

"Neto. You said solitary wasn't so bad because you had him around—and it pissed me off."

"I don't think I ever said it 'wasn't so bad,' but…really? I didn't even realize you felt that way about Neto."

"You're just too dense."

"That's not true. Dick, you're the one who doesn't show your emotions enough."

Though he said that, thinking back, Yuuto realized it made sense. When Yuuto fell sick with a fever right after leaving solitary, Dick had mentioned Neto's name first, and he did seem angry, but until that moment, he had never realized that it was jealousy.

"Neto is a friend. I really like him, but I don't feel anything beyond friendship."

"Yeah, I know. It's just stupid jealousy, don't worry about it."

"You went to L.A. to see Neto, didn't you?" The thought of Jim Faber, who was murdered, crossed Yuuto's mind. He wondered if Dick was involved but chose not to ask—he didn't want to shatter this brief moment of happiness. "You ran away from me back then.

Did you really not want to see me that badly?"

He thought it was childish to ask now, but the bitter words slipped out anyway.

"Of course, I ran. I knew what would happen if I saw you. I'm scared of you."

"Scared?" The unexpected words took aback Yuuto. There was nothing less fitting for Dick than the word *scared.*

"Yeah. You're the most dangerous person to me."

Just as Yuuto was about to ask what he meant by that, there was a knock at the door.

Room service had arrived.

Dick answered the door in his bathrobe and returned with a tray holding pizza and a bottle of olive oil. Setting the tray on the table, he didn't spare the food a glance. Instead, he took up the olive oil and strode back to Yuuto.

"Lie down on your stomach."

CHAPTER 17

Dick sat down at the edge of the bed while opening the bottle. Yuuto obediently lay on his stomach, turning his vulnerable back toward Dick. Cool oil dripped generously down from his waist, and his body twitched.

"Cold?" Dick asked. "Hang on. I'll warm you up soon."

Dick's hands gently massaged, kneading Yuuto's buttocks as if to soothe away all tension. Yuuto hugged his pillow tightly, wrapped in a mixture of comfort and embarrassment.

Dick's fingers traced back and forth over Yuuto's crack. Every time the sensitive spot was softly touched, Yuuto tensed reflexively, but Dick patiently waited for him to relax.

When Yuuto finally began to relax, Dick lay down beside him. Facing each other on their sides, Dick's touch grew slow and tender as he caressed him. Yuuto hooked a leg over Dick's hip, soft moans slipping past his lips.

While planting slow, sweet kisses, Dick slid a finger inside. The tight, closed opening had completely loosened, softly swallowing his long finger to the base.

"Does it hurt?"

"No…it's fine…"

Even when Dick added a second finger, Yuuto felt no pain. Instead, the sensation of rubbing deep inside started to feel good.

"If it's too much, just tell me. I'll stop right away."

Yuuto appreciated Dick's kindness and care. He had always been like this. Despite his cold exterior, Dick genuinely cared for him. He was truly a loving man.

That this gentle man was now living only for revenge made Yuuto's chest ache. He felt sad watching Dick lock away his overflowing kindness and force himself to be ruthless. Yuuto wished with all his heart that Dick could choose an easier way to live.

Friendship, pity, or love—it no longer mattered. This swelling affection needed no label. Yuuto simply loved the man called Dick. He loved him more than anyone else and wished with all his heart for his happiness. He prayed for it, desperately so.

"Ah! Fu—" Two fingers pressed hard against a part of the inner wall. A trembling, deep pleasure welled up inside Yuuto, and he shook his head lightly. "Not there…no…"

"You mean, 'that's the spot,' right? You're practically melting. Feels like I could fit my whole fist in there, want to try?"

"Don't say weird things," Yuuto turned over and faced away from Dick.

"Hey, are you mad? That was a joke." Dick quickly apologized, surprised by Yuuto's sudden turn of his back. The way Dick hurriedly tried to explain was so endearing that Yuuto smiled, pressing his cheek into the sheets.

"I'm not angry—I was telling you to hurry up and get over here. Got the message?"

Dick sighed in relief and wrapped his arms around Yuuto's back. "Relax."

At Dick's whisper, Yuuto lay face down again, parting his legs and lifting his hips slightly to make it easier. He could feel the burning length pressing into his slick heat, slowly sliding deeper and deeper.

"*Ah…*" The pain was bearable, yet the sheer thickness stole his breath away. It was so much more than his fingers.

"Can I move? Or is it still too much?"

"Move…yeah. Let me feel more of you."

Dick's length seemed to revel in finally being welcomed back into Yuuto after so long a deprivation. He drove into the tight heat without pause, thrusting in and out with unrestrained vigor.

Dick lifted Yuuto's hips, shifting him onto all fours before driving deep inside. He pushed in to the hilt, then drew back slowly, only to repeat the motion again and again until Yuuto's arms gave out. His cheek pressed to the sheets, hips raised in a helplessly shameful posture, he could only take the force of Dick's relentless thrusts.

"Yuuto…Yuuto…" Dick shifted his hips and repeatedly called Yuuto's name in a hoarse voice.

Usually calm and collected, Dick was lost in his passion, devouring Yuuto. The thought made Yuuto happier than anything. He wanted Dick to drown in this, to lose himself completely, and only in him.

"Dick, yes…more…deeper…!" The intensity was almost painful, but Yuuto wanted to tease Dick, so he whispered words of invitation.

"More? You sure about that, Yuuto? If I go any further, I might break you."

"I want that. Break me…please, break me."

When Dick paused, impatience got the better of Yuuto. He rolled his hips back against him, his slick, narrow opening drawing in the thick length with wet, obscene sounds. "Come on…fuck me…I want you… please, Dick…"

Yuuto sniffled through his tears as he begged, raw and unguarded. All he wanted was for Dick to love him so fiercely he couldn't think of anything else. He wanted them both to surrender to their animal instincts, to fall together as far as they could go.

"Yuuto…My sweet, sweet Yuuto."

Dick's hands clamped tight around Yuuto's hips as he drove

into him with furious thrusts. The violent pace left Yuuto reeling, dizziness clouding his senses. He bit down hard, clenching his teeth to keep from biting his own tongue.

Pleasure and pain blurred together until Yuuto couldn't even distinguish what he was feeling anymore. But he was happy, truly happy. Just knowing Dick wanted him, that they were one, was enough.

"*Ah!*"

Yuuto heard Dick's groan, and in that instant—knowing the man he loved had reached his peak—he let his own consciousness slip away, overwhelmed by a profound sense of fulfillment.

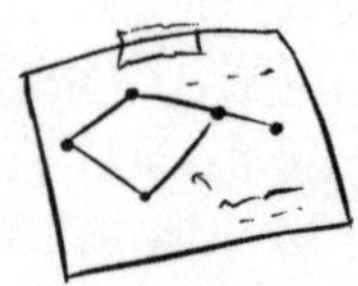

"Yuuto, Yuuto—" The feeling of someone repeatedly patting his cheek pulled Yuuto back to consciousness. When he opened his eyes, he saw Dick leaning over him, looking concerned. "You okay?"

"What happened?" Still disoriented, Yuuto stared blankly at Dick's face, unable to understand what was going on.

"You passed out." Dick looked truly remorseful as he gave a gentle kiss to Yuuto's forehead. "Sorry. I pushed you too hard."

"It's not your fault. I was the one who provoked you."

"Even so, I was an idiot. No matter how worked up I was, I shouldn't have lost control like that."

The sight of Dick looking so dejected was strangely endearing, leaving Yuuto with a bittersweet ache in his chest. He raised a heavy arm and wrapped it around Dick's head, pulling him against his chest.

"I was happy," Yuuto murmured. "You were so caught up in

me that you forgot yourself."

Burying his nose in Yuuto's neck, Dick whispered, "Let me make it up to you."

"Make it up to me?"

"Yeah. You didn't come, did you? This time, I'll be gentle… okay?"

Yuuto had no reason to turn down a second invitation. He smiled faintly and was about to nod when a sharp ringtone suddenly sliced through the room.

"My phone," Dick said, sitting up. He grabbed his phone from the writing desk. "Hey, Jessica?"

Yuuto's body went rigid at those words.

"Ah…no. I see. Got it. Thanks. I'll be there soon." When Dick hung up, his expression was tense.

Yuuto understood immediately. Reality had come knocking. Their showtime was over. It was the curtain call on a blissful night.

"Yuuto—"

"I know," Yuuto said softly, cutting him off. He pushed himself up and got out of bed. "Do I have time to take a shower?"

"Yeah. Yuuto, I'm sorry. Jessica's at the hotel bar drinking with Eagan, and she asked me to come join them."

Eagan was Dick's target. There was no way he'd let an opportunity like that slip by.

"You don't have to explain it to me. I'll make it quick—five minutes."

Still naked, Yuuto headed to the bathroom and scrubbed away every trace of their intimacy under the hot shower spray. He should have felt sad, but instead, his heart felt parched and numb. Mechanically, he dried off and went back to the room, where Dick—already dressed—sat waiting on the bed. Yuuto's suit had been neatly hung on a hanger by Dick.

Once they were ready, Dick exited the room with him. The air was thick between them, and neither of them dared to meet the other's gaze.

"I'm going up. You take this one first," Dick said, pressing the elevator button and motioning for Yuuto to step in.

Yuuto entered the elevator alone and pressed the first-floor button. Was this really it? Was this the end?

Just as the doors started to close, Yuuto's hand shot out and pressed the "Open" button. He couldn't just walk away like this. He couldn't leave without saying something, anything. The doors slid open again, and they stared at each other, Yuuto from inside the elevator, Dick from the hallway.

"Dick. If…if I said I was going to quit the FBI and help you, what would you say?"

Dick stood frozen, his expression unreadable. Yuuto didn't move either, waiting for his answer.

The words slipped out before Yuuto even realized what he was saying, but he meant every one of them. If by some chance Dick wanted it, he was willing to give his life for him. If Dick asked him to stay by his side, he would abandon everything else without hesitation.

"You couldn't," Dick said with a wan smile, a shadow of sadness flickering in it. "You could never live the way I do."

"That's not true. If you wanted me to, I'd do anything—"

Dick stepped closer, softly touching Yuuto's cheek. "You're not that kind of man. If you were the type to live selfishly, only thinking of yourself, then back when I asked you to run away with me, you would have gone without hesitation."

"Dick…"

"You're not the type of man who can live by doing the wrong thing," Dick said softly. "You have pride as an agent. Even if I was the reason you joined the FBI, you could never abandon the work you've been assigned, could you? As a man, as someone determined to live honestly, I respect you with everything I have. That's why you don't need to throw anything away for someone like me."

"But, Dick…I-I—" Yuuto's breath hitched, cutting off his words. He grabbed Dick's hand where it rested against his cheek. Just then, he heard footsteps coming down the hall.

"Someone's coming. Go," Dick whispered, pulling away. His clear eyes held steady as he added, "From this moment on, you and I are enemies."

"Dick…"

"We're chasing the same target for different reasons. Of course we'll be on opposite sides. But that doesn't mean we have to hate each other."

The detached way he said it cut deeper than any cruel words ever could. If only Dick had told him to hate him, it might have been easier. Crushed, Yuuto let go of the button holding the elevator doors open. Slowly, they slid shut, hiding Dick's face from view.

"Damn it!"

Yuuto hit the wall of the descending elevator and covered his mouth with a hand. If he didn't, he was afraid a useless cry would escape. In the small metal box, quiet, broken sobs spilled out, sobs no one would ever hear.

When he got back to his hotel and stopped by the front desk, the clerk said, "We already gave the key to your roommate," and Yuuto realized Rob was back.

He slipped into the lobby bathroom and glanced at his reflection in the mirror. His eyes were a bit red, but not enough for anyone to notice. Convinced he could hide it, Yuuto made his way back to his room.

When he knocked, Rob opened the door—tie already discarded, dress shirt hanging loosely on his frame.

"Welcome back. You were out, huh?"

"Yeah. You're back early, Rob. I thought you'd be out later than this."

"I wrapped it up early. If I'd stuck around with those guys any longer, we'd have been there till morning."

Yuuto hung his jacket on a hanger and sat down on the bed. Rob, for some reason, leaned against the wall with his arms crossed, watching him.

"What?"

"Nothing. You just look tired."

"Do I?" Yuuto gave a wry smile and rubbed his face with his right hand.

Rob walked over and sat down right next to him. "You saw Dick, didn't you?"

Yuuto's heart clenched tightly, and his shoulders quivered faintly.

"That Steve Müeller we met today…He's the Dick you've been looking for, isn't he?

"How did you…?" Yuuto stared at Rob in disbelief, clenching his hands to hide his unease.

"The look on your face when you saw him—it all clicked. You looked like a man who'd just found his long-lost twin," Rob said. "So? Did you talk to him? Did you figure out how you really feel?"

"Rob…"

Rob's voice wasn't accusatory; it was gentle and comforting. That kindness completely unraveled Yuuto. Maybe it was because, in front of Rob—who already knew everything—he didn't have to pretend anymore.

"What's wrong? You look like you're about to cry. Don't tell me… did he turn you away?"

"No…no, it's not like that. At first, he did reject me, but…only because it was hard for him too. And then…I realized he felt the same way I do, and I—" His words faltered, breaking apart. He couldn't go on. He hadn't even had time to process everything that had happened tonight.

Rob gently rubbed Yuuto's back in slow, soothing circles, calming him down. "Take your time. You don't need to pick the right words."

Gradually, Yuuto's breathing became steadier. Maybe speaking out loud would help him understand his feelings. With that idea, he started to talk, to put into words the certainty that had taken hold in his mind.

"When he stood in front of me, my mind went blank. I wasn't mistaken, and I wasn't imagining things. I knew then—and I know now—that I love Dick."

"If that's what you've decided, then I won't say anything else," Rob murmured, his hand brushing over Yuuto's still-damp hair. "You showered, so I'm guessing you spent some happy time with him, huh?"

"But I think it's only made things harder," Yuuto admitted. "Even if I know for sure that I love him, nothing between us can change. I'm trying to arrest Corvus, and Dick's trying to kill him. We're practically enemies."

Rob looked at Yuuto's profile for a moment, then spoke in a calm voice. "You know…I've been thinking."

"Huh?"

"At the risk of saying something you might not like, can I be honest with you?"

Yuuto nodded. Whatever Rob had to say—even if it hurt—he wanted to hear it.

"Right now, Yuuto…I think you're stuck in the middle," Rob said plainly.

CHAPTER 18

Yuuto blinked at Rob.

"What do you mean?"

"You joined the FBI because you wanted to see Dick again. Of course, I'm not saying you've been slacking off—you've been serious about the job, and I know you're committed to the investigation. But…" Rob gave him a pointed look. "Deep down, isn't there a part of you that doesn't want to get in Dick's way?"

"That's…"

"Right now, your sympathy for him is too strong. I understand why he wants revenge on the man who killed his partner. I get it. But you're an FBI agent, Yuuto. No matter the reason, you can't condone murder. You can't just accept what Dick's trying to do."

"I'm not blindly accepting it. I just…" Yuuto shook his head, flustered. "I understand how much it hurts him, and—"

"Understanding is fine," Rob interrupted. "But agreeing with him isn't. You need to adopt the mindset that you'll stop him yourself if it comes to that. Otherwise, you'll keep wavering, torn between your feelings for Dick and your duty as an agent. You'll never move forward like that."

Rob was right. Yuuto had known it all along, but kept looking away from it.

If he were the one to find and arrest Corvus first, it would mean standing in Dick's way. Yet he'd always told himself, almost as an excuse, that arresting Corvus wasn't about obstructing Dick's revenge—it was simply the natural result of his duty.

"Your original goal was just to see Dick again," Rob continued. "Now that you've done that, ask yourself what your purpose is moving forward and what resolve you're willing to hold onto. If you don't, you'll eventually hit a wall."

As Yuuto drifted into thought, Rob got up from the bed. "I'm gonna take a shower."

Left alone, Yuuto sat there, replaying Rob's words in his mind.

The reason he'd joined the FBI was entirely personal. But somewhere along the way, while chasing Corvus, something inside him had changed. Now, he truly wanted to catch Corvus himself—wanted to bring him down.

His personal feelings and his duty as an agent…

Rob was right. If he didn't separate them now, it would only get more dangerous.

Even after Rob had fallen asleep, Yuuto stayed seated on the bed, gazing into the darkness of the room as he confronted the turmoil within his own heart.

He had always wanted to be the one who understood Dick better than anyone else. Yet he couldn't deny that part of it was selfish—a fear of being disliked, of becoming someone Dick might find bothersome. More than anything, he didn't want Dick to hate him. Those feelings had weighed on him all this time, dragging him down.

Although Yuuto had no intention of condoning murder, a part of him still wanted to help Dick fulfill his wish. He had always felt he had no right to interfere with Dick's mission—an earnest resolve to which the man had devoted every fiber of his being.

But was wishing for Dick's happiness truly the same as letting him take Corvus's life?

Would killing Corvus really make Dick happy?

Maybe, in that moment, when he finally stopped Corvus's breathing, Dick would feel a deep, fleeting sense of satisfaction.

Perhaps he'd revel in the achievement, believing he had avenged his fallen comrades.

But that kind of joy could never last. Dick must have known that himself. He wasn't a man who lashed out recklessly in blind rage. He was calm, controlled, relentlessly focused on his pursuit of Corvus. A man like that couldn't possibly be unaware of the future awaiting him.

The moment he killed Corvus…he would lose his reason for living.

A shiver ran down Yuuto's spine. He wrapped his arms around his shoulders as if to hold himself together.

Ordinary people didn't need a reason to live. People didn't survive because they had some grand purpose—they lived simply because they were alive. They carried on because life was natural and self-sustaining, and they didn't question it.

But Dick…Dick needed a reason.

Yuuto thought about the darkness in Dick's heart. He had lost his team—his family—and the man he loved right in front of him. Corvus had planted a bomb, killing them all in an instant.

Dick, who had grown up as an orphan, finally found a family at the end of a long, lonely road. Among them was a kind, older man who taught him what it meant to love.

And then, in a single, horrific moment, all of them were reduced to lifeless, broken flesh. Yuuto shuddered as he pictured the scene. What had Dick felt at that moment? What had he thought while staring at the blood of the people he loved most?

I should've died with them. Dick's words echoed in Yuuto's mind.

Perhaps the worst part of his suffering was that he had survived when no one else did. Maybe the only thing allowing him to go on now was his relentless pursuit of revenge.

And if that was true…

Once Dick killed Corvus, he might also end his own life. Satisfied that he had completed his mission, he might finally join the people he had lost.

It was just Yuuto's guess, but it seemed very likely. For Dick, his life now felt like nothing more than a suspended sentence. Not only Corvus, but Dick himself was trapped in a deep, endless darkness.

Beyond the curtains, the sky was beginning to pale with the first light of dawn.

Night would always yield to morning as long as one lived, yet that light never touched Dick's heart. He had turned away from it, condemned to struggle and suffer in darkness.

Yuuto slid out of bed and walked to the window. He pulled the curtain back just enough to look out at the dawn sky, painted in soft shades of violet. It was so beautiful it felt as if it could wash his soul clean, as though every bit of the darkness clinging to him might simply dissolve.

Between the buildings, the sun rose, its new rays spilling across the city and warming Yuuto's skin.

If only that light could reach Dick's heart as well.

With that heavy thought in his mind, Yuuto pressed his forehead against the glass.

He slightly narrowed his eyes, watching quietly with reverence as a new day started.

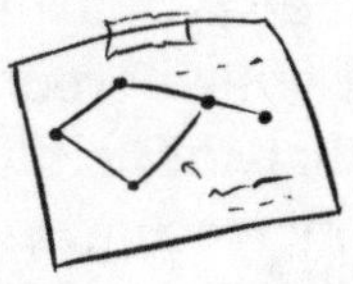

"Didn't you sleep at all last night?" Rob asked as he ate a strip of bacon during breakfast at the hotel restaurant. "I saw you standing by the window at dawn. Was it because of something I said that you couldn't sleep?"

"I appreciated what you said, Rob. I figured it was a good opportunity, so I decided to think everything through," Yuuto replied. He set his coffee cup down and smiled at Rob.

"Did you find an answer?"

"Yeah. Somehow."

Rob only nodded with a quiet, "I see," before returning to his meal. He didn't ask for Yuuto's answer, perhaps because he already knew. Today, Yuuto seemed lighter, as if a weight had finally been lifted from his shoulders, his expression clear and refreshed.

"By the way," Rob continued, "yesterday I heard something from a friend who knows a lot about the defense industry. Apparently, President Eagan of Smith-Bucks Company is the nephew of the president of General Mars. I didn't know that myself, so it surprised me."

"Huh. So they keep the executive board in the family."

"And if that wasn't enough, the president of General Mars? His daughter is married to Bill Manning."

"Manning? The vice-presidential candidate?"

"Yeah. And to add to that, the Manning family has been lining their pockets in the oil business for years. They have deep connections with Middle Eastern countries. Naturally, they're tied hand in glove with the defense industry."

It was widely rumored that the munitions industry and oil capital were constant forces behind the government. The close ties between officials and arms corporations were a well-known example. Many argued that those bloated conglomerates were driving the United States' increasing military interventions abroad.

Rob glanced around, ensuring no other guests were sitting close enough to overhear, before lowering his voice.

"Yuuto, I can't shake the feeling that White Heaven has some kind of tie to the government. I can't say what the connection is, but… you've heard of the Iran–Contra affair, right?"

"Of course. That political scandal from the 1980s."

The United States government secretly sold weapons to Iran, its enemy at the time, and used the profits to fund the Contra rebels in Nicaragua by supplying them with arms. When the scheme was exposed, it became a national scandal.

"America claimed to support the anti-Communist Contras, but it was the CIA that had created them in the first place. Backed fully by the Agency, they carried out guerrilla operations that fueled civil unrest. Publicly, the U.S. government staged a show of denouncing terrorism, yet in truth, the CIA had pulled the strings in nearly every coup d'état across Latin America. Terrorism, in many ways, was one of America's specialties."

As Yuuto listened to Rob's words, he drifted into thought again. What Rob said wasn't wrong. In the past, the United States had indeed interfered unfairly in Central and South America. However, White Heaven's targets were located within the United States itself. It was hard to believe White Heaven was connected to a political conspiracy.

When Yuuto voiced his doubt, Rob gave a wry smile.

"Have you heard of Operation Northwoods, proposed in 1962 by the military and the CIA? The plan involved staging bombings in several locations within the United States, making it appear as if Cuban agents were responsible, all to justify a military invasion of Cuba. They even thought about disguising military planes as civilian aircraft, blowing them up midair, and then claiming Cuba had attacked us. President Kennedy rejected this plan, so it never happened, but the U.S. government has plenty of other false-flag incidents. Pearl Harbor was one of them. They knew the Japanese attack was coming, but didn't stop it. Many in the public were against going to war, so the U.S. couldn't declare it—until after Pearl Harbor, when public opinion shifted sharply in favor."

"That story isn't confirmed, though," Yuuto said, taking a sip of his now-cold coffee as he waited for Rob's reply.

"I don't trust the United States government at all. They're the kind of people who'll do whatever it takes—no matter how despicable—to sway public opinion."

But if White Heaven is linked to the government, then why would the CIA try to eliminate Corvus? The CIA should follow the government's orders. Isn't that contradictory?"

"That's the mystery. But White Heaven isn't simply a cult. That much is clear."

A customer sat in the seat next to them, so Rob ended the grim conversation.

After finishing their meal and getting ready to leave the restaurant, Rob stopped by a tapestry hanging near the entrance. It featured a stylish design inspired by constellations, and Rob looked at it with enthusiasm.

"This is nice," he said. "I've wanted something like this for my room."

"Do you like constellations?" Yuuto asked.

"Not exactly, but there's something kind of mystical about them, don't you think?"

Once they stepped out into the hallway, Yuuto remembered something from his childhood. He had become fascinated with a telescope his father had bought him and spent a period staring at the sky with intense curiosity. Back then, he'd studied constellation guides and even developed a strong interest in the Greek myths behind the star patterns.

When Yuuto mentioned this, Rob nodded in agreement. "Greek mythology is pretty fascinating."

"Speaking of which, the constellation Corvus is named after a raven, even though it means crow, right? That one has a story, too."

"Yeah. The crow was originally a beautiful bird with silver feathers that could speak human language," Yuuto recounted. "But after lying and angering Apollo, its feathers turned black, and it lost the power of speech. Then, as a punishment, it was nailed to the sky."

Corvus, or Corvi by its scientific name—sometimes called The Raven—was one of Ptolemy's forty-eight constellations.

"That's the one. Crows have always been a little hated, haven't they?" Rob said, then added, "It's a simple constellation—I don't know much about it. What stars does it have again?"

"If I remember right, the Alpha star was called Alchiba, which means 'tent' in Arabic—" Yuuto answered without thinking—then jolted as if struck by lightning at the sound of his own words. "The Alpha Corvi star, Rob…"

"Huh? Alpha star means the brightest main star in a constellation, right? What about it?"

"The 'Alpha' Corvus mentioned! That was Alchiba!"

CHAPTER 19

Rob looked completely confused, staring at the excited Yuuto with a blank expression. Wanting to avoid explaining further, Yuuto grabbed Rob's arm and pulled him forward.

"Hey, hey, where are you going?"

"To the business center. It's on the first floor, isn't it?"

Yuuto rushed into the business center tucked in a corner of the lobby and sat down at a free computer. He typed in "Corvus constellation" and found a flood of pages. One site had a photo of the constellation shaped like a crow.

"This is it." Yuuto printed the image on the computer's printer and handed it to Rob. "Look at it sideways. It's the same shape, isn't it?"

Viewed that way, with the crow's head pointing downward, the constellation formed a vertically elongated trapezoid. But when rotated ninety degrees counterclockwise, the shape of the constellation matched the locations of the consecutive bombing incidents perfectly.

"It's true. They really do look alike…Let's compare it to the map right away." Rob's excitement was plain in his voice. The two hurried back to their room, opened the file, and spread out the map. Placing the constellation image beside it, they saw the shapes lined up perfectly.

"This is incredible, Yuuto. It matches perfectly. Epsilon star is Michigan, Beta star is Florida, Gamma star is Montana, Delta star is Utah, Eta star is Arizona. Corvus placed the bombs according to the positions of the stars in the Corvus constellation."

"So, the last remaining Alpha star…where would that be on this map?"

Rob traced the position of the Alpha star on the map with a marker, ensuring it matched the constellation's scale. "Yeah. It's roughly around here."

Yuuto stared at the map, speechless. Of all places, it was the worst possible target.

"Corvus's next target is New York?"

Rob's mark was near Manhattan. "There might be some margin of error, so it's not absolute, but if it's here, this would be a fitting place for the final strike, don't you think?"

Recalling the enormous stash of plastic explosives he'd seen at the Japanese American National Museum, Yuuto shuddered. Manhattan was the most densely populated urban area in the United States. Skyscrapers covered the entire island, and it was said that eighty percent of New York City's workforce had their jobs there. If a massive explosion were to occur in such a place, the damage would be devastating.

"We should go to the FBI headquarters right now and inform Heiden about this—"

Rob was interrupted by the ring of the hotel phone. Yuuto picked it up—the front desk said there was an outside call for Rob.

Taking the receiver, Rob listened intently, his brow furrowing as he answered with the occasional, 'mm-hmm,' to the voice on the other end.

"Understood. We'll wait in front of the hotel."

After hanging up, Rob gave Yuuto a confused look.

"Who was that?"

"President Eagan's secretary. Apparently, the president wants to speak with us and asked that we come to the hotel. They said a car will be sent to pick us up soon, so we should wait."

"I wonder what it's about. Judging by yesterday's attitude, it seemed like there was nothing left to say."

"Well, let's go. Contact with Eagan probably won't do us any harm."

After a short while, the two left their room. Standing by the hotel's driveway, they waited until a man in a black suit approached them. Although it wasn't especially cold, he wore a trench coat draped over his arm.

"Are you Dr. Connors?" The tall man with a hooked nose nodded in response when Rob confirmed. He introduced himself as an employee of Smith-Bucks Company and led them toward the street. "Apologies. I left the car parked just a little farther ahead."

The man was polite enough, but something about him felt phony to Yuuto. He claimed to be picking up clients on the president's orders, yet made them walk. Ordinarily, he should have circled back, brought the car around, and parked right in front of the hotel.

"There it is." The man pointed at a black sedan with its hazard lights flashing. Another man sat in the driver's seat. Yuuto's uneasy feeling intensified.

"Please." The man opened the rear door and gestured for them to get in.

Without hesitation, Rob began to climb inside, but Yuuto grabbed his arm and stopped him. "Rob, don't get in."

"Huh?"

"I forgot something back at the hotel. Could you wait for a moment?"

As Yuuto pulled Rob back, the man's expression changed instantly. His friendly smile disappeared, replaced by a sharp, piercing glare directed at both of them.

"You're not going back to the hotel. Get in quietly." The

command was cold and stern.

Rob frowned. “That’s rude—” His words cut off as his face went rigid. From beneath the man’s trench coat, the barrel of a gun glinted into view.

“Get in the car. Quickly. Try anything, and I’ll shoot.

Yuuto raised both hands slightly and said, “O-okay. I’ll cooperate, so don’t point that at me.”

Feigning fear, Yuuto rushed toward the car—but it was only an act. As he leaned inside, his hand darted beneath the man’s jacket. In one swift motion, he drew the SIG Sauer P226 from the shoulder holster and spun, pressing the muzzle hard against the man’s chest, aimed straight at his heart.

The man’s face twitched, and he gasped sharply. Yuuto pressed the muzzle harder while his left hand slid beneath the trench coat to grab another pistol. He slipped it into his belt and demanded sharply, “Who sent you? Eagan?”

The man turned pale but kept his lips sealed, refusing to answer. At that moment, Rob shouted, “Watch out!” while looking toward the driver’s seat.

The man driving aimed his gun at Yuuto and pulled the trigger.

Yuuto dropped to the ground just in time, avoiding the shot. But that movement freed the man he’d been holding, who slipped into the car. It seemed the man had a second gun because, from the back window, he fired several rounds at Yuuto and Rob.

Gunshots rang out loudly as nearby pedestrians screamed and crouched in fear. A firefight in a place like this would inevitably put innocent bystanders at risk.

Yuuto grabbed Rob’s arm, and they ran. The car’s tires screeched as it gave chase.

“Yuuto, they’re catching up! We should dive into a building or something…”

“No, that’ll just trap us like rats in a cage.”

Yuuto and Rob reached a crossroads and, without slowing down, tried to cross the intersection. But a white sedan suddenly cut in front of them, slamming on the brakes right on the crosswalk.

Just as Yuuto cursed their luck, a man wearing black sunglasses appeared at the driver's side window, shouting at them. "Get in the car!"

Yuuto's eyes went wide in shock at the unexpected sight. "Dick?"

"What are you doing, Yuuto? Hurry up!"

There was no mistaking it—this was Dick. Coming back to reality, Yuuto opened the rear door and pushed Rob inside. As Yuuto climbed in and shut the door, Dick hit the accelerator hard and sped away through the city at a furious pace.

"They're chasing us!" Rob shouted, looking back. The black sedan was tailing them recklessly, running red lights. The man in the passenger seat leaned out the window.

Seeing that, Yuuto pushed Rob down with his whole body. Just then, a loud crash echoed behind them, and the rear window shattered in a spiderweb pattern.

"They're serious about this," Dick muttered darkly, pressing down on the gas even harder. Dick weaved aggressively through traffic at breakneck speed, drawing angry honks from surrounding drivers. "Hold on tight. Once we lose them, I'll get you to the FBI headquarters."

"Dick, watch out!" Yuuto yelled in alarm. As they raced through the intersection, the light changed from green to red—and a huge tractor-trailer sped in from the right.

"We're gonna hit it!" Rob shouted. The giant truck approached steadily, blocking the intersection.

There was no way to avoid it!

Yuuto gripped the seat in front of him, bracing for impact. But instead of braking, Dick slammed on the gas and swerved to cut in front of the trailer. In the back seat, Yuuto and Rob were tossed side to side like ragdolls.

With just inches to spare from a collision, Dick skillfully squeezed past the truck—an incredible, near-miraculous maneuver.

"Whew." Rob exhaled in relief. Looking back, he saw the intersection was blocked not just by the trailer but also by other cars trapped in a chaotic pileup.

From the looks of it, none of those cars would be moving anytime soon. The black sedan was blocked in by the truck, no doubt leaving its occupants gnashing their teeth in frustration, trapped with nowhere to go—forward or back.

"Looks like we're safe for now." Dick finally slowed down.

Rob shook his head and muttered, "Never thought I'd experience a car chase in D.C."

"Dick. Why did you show up there like that?"

Dick's timely arrival had rescued them, but it seemed almost too convenient to be just a coincidence.

"I was tailing that black sedan. I never expected they were targeting you two."

"Those guys claimed they worked for Smith-Bucks Company, right?"

Dick gave an ambiguous answer. "I can't say they're completely unrelated. But it wasn't Eagan who sent them after you. That man doesn't have that kind of guts."

The car pulled up at the FBI headquarters. Yuuto and Rob got out.

"Thanks, Dick."

Still holding the steering wheel, Dick took off his sunglasses. Their eyes met, and Yuuto felt a painful reminder of last night's events. But he resolved not to reveal his personal feelings at this time.

"Be careful."

"You too. The deeper you dig into Corvus's shadows, the more dangerous it gets."

Yuuto nodded and looked Dick straight in the eyes. "Dick, there's one thing I want to say."

He knew he had to say it now; the chance might not come again.

"What is it?"

"I'm going to find Corvus before you do. I won't let you kill him. I'll arrest him first and make sure he faces justice under the law."

Even as he said it, unease twisted in his chest. It sounded like a declaration of war, and he knew Dick might take it that way. But Yuuto had made up his mind. Not out of hostility, but because he cared for Dick, he would catch Corvus with his own hands. He wouldn't let Dick's hands be stained with Corvus's blood.

From this point forward, he would set aside his personal feelings and pursue Corvus solely as an investigator.

"You should follow the path you believe in."

There was no anger in Dick's eyes. No sadness, no irritation, no resignation, nothing at all. His unwavering blue eyes resembled a lake at the edge of the world. A pebble tossed in produced no ripples. It simply sank beneath the surface in silence.

Just as Yuuto had spent the night making a decision, maybe Dick had also resolved something deep inside.

"I was always afraid of you," Dick said. "You were the only one who unsettled my heart, made my resolve waver. But I've finally let it go. Just as you're going to follow your path, I'll follow mine."

"Dick…"

The connection between them had once been broken at

Schelger Prison, and now, 2,800 miles away, fate had strangely brought them back together. But that bond was unraveling again. Still, this was their decision. No one had forced them to do so. They chose to part ways on their own terms.

Yuuto silently spoke to Dick in his heart. *If you're trapped in a lonely battle, then I'll plunge into that loneliness with you. If you've chosen to chase Corvus as though possessed by his curse, then I'll chase him as though in prayer—even if it means you'll come to hate me.*

"Yuuto, listen carefully," Dick said as he released the handbrake. "Move cautiously. If you slip up, you'll be buried before you can flush out Corvus. They won't show an ounce of mercy, even if their opponent is the FBI."

Yuuto couldn't help but ask back, startled. "They? You mean Smith-Bucks Company?"

Dick shook his head and put his sunglasses back on. "Your real enemy is the monster inside the White House."

The White House?

At that moment, Yuuto lost his words as Dick suddenly sped off.

"Dick…!"

He watched the white sedan get smaller and smaller in the distance. Yuuto could only stand there in stunned silence, watching him disappear down the street.

AFTERWORD

Hello, this is Aida. This is my second book with Chara Bunko. This book is the sequel to *DEADLOCK*, which was released last September. If you haven't read the previous work, be sure to check out the story about Yuuto and Dick's first meeting.

The setting of the previous work was a prison. Since I enjoy prison stories, I personally liked writing it, but I was a bit anxious about whether readers would accept it.

However, the readers were very open-minded, and I received many comments saying they found it interesting. I was so relieved I nearly cried, and at that moment, I rented some prison movies I had been curious about for a while. Watching them, I was moved to tears thinking, "Prison movies really are the best!" and then I started writing the sequel.

Putting my prison obsession aside, the highlight this time is the love scene on a clean bed that Dick had long wished for. Dick Burnford (a pseudonym), the guy who orders pizza for sex...

Additionally, Neto, a character readers passionately supported in the previous book, returns. Since I received many love calls asking to bring him back, it's a cameo appearance. As usual, he's a man who's sweet only to Yuuto. More than a friend now, he's become like a worried father watching over his daughter.

The new character, Rob, has a subtle role (laughs). Still, despite his light-hearted vibe, he's quite reliable when it comes to advancing the investigation, so it seems he will continue supporting Yuuto in the next book as well.

Once again, many thanks to Yuh Takashina for the illustrations. Thank you very much for another wonderful cover! Sexy pose (?) Yuuto and Dick are dressed in suits and glasses. Both are so handsome you can't look away. I don't know how many times your incredible illustrations have saved me. I am truly grateful. Please continue to support me with the next book as well.

To my editor M, I'm truly sorry for causing so much trouble again this time. Despite the difficult situation, you always encouraged me brightly with "Let's do good work," and because of that, I was able to stay motivated and keep writing.

Thank you very much.

By the way, the word "deadheat" used in this title is often used in Japan to describe intense races or close contests. However, originally, in English, it means a tie, a draw, or a match without a winner. The latter meaning feels more fitting for the image of this work.

The CIA and FBI. Those who attempt to kill and those who try to arrest. Yuuto and Dick have each taken their own path and parted ways again, but this story will conclude in the third book.

Please read until the very end to see how the relationship between the two chasing Corvus will unfold.

February 2007

Saki Aida

The story continues in

DEADSHOT

A Deadlock Novel

FEDERAL BUREAU OF INVESTIGATION
DEPARTMENT OF JUSTICE
FEDERAL BUREAU OF INVESTIGATION
FBI
SPECIAL AGENT
YUUTO LENNIX
SSA
Deadlock Volume 3
DEADSHOT

BLOVED PUBLISHING